Mountain of Death

ALAN C. PORTER

A Black Horse Western

ROBERT HALE · LONDON

Typeset by
Derek Doyle & Associates, Liverpool.
Printed and bound in Great Britain by
Antony Rowe Limited, Wiltshire

CHAPTER 1

The lightning flashed. A vivid, sizzling whiteness that made the boy jump. It was followed almost immediately by an explosive rumble of thunder that seemed to make the very mountain shake and the boy gave a whimper of fear. Outside the cave amid the crags and high peaks the rain, driven to a frenzy by the howling wind, lashed the rocks and filled ravines with foaming, boiling cataracts of water that in turn fell in majestic, white shrouds from high ledges into deep valleys.

In the storm-riven darkness of the night the boy could see none of the savage, awesome beauty of the tumbling falls and foaming rivers, only hear the maniacal laugh of the thunder echoing in hidden tunnels and undiscovered caverns of Hollow Mountain.

Lightning flashed again beyond the cave entrance, turning the rain into needles of silver. The boy sat close to a small fire, peering fearfully back over his shoulder. Across from him a big, genial-faced man looked up and chuckled.

'Just mother nature, boy, ain't no need to fret,' he soothed. 'She'll blow hersel' out by dawn.'

'Yes, Pa,' the boy said doubtfully. The storm had taken them by surprise, but luck had been on their side. They had come upon the cave as the first wave of rain had begun lashing down. It was big and roomy. Enough room for them and the horse and pony they had been riding to shelter in, and as an added bonus the cave floor was scattered with bone-dry twigs and branches, making it possible for the man to light the fire. The man surmised they had been dragged in by some animal in the past. Towards the rear of the cave the floor fell away into a shaft that dropped down sheer into the very bowels of the mountain. The man had warned the boy to keep away from it.

The horse and pony whickered nervously and nuzzled each other for comfort, but they had trust in the big man and the boy and the voice of either could sooth them.

'Ain't there supposed to be ghosts an' demons up here, Pa?' the boy asked nervously and the man laughed: a booming, comforting sound.

'Bless you, boy, you've been listening to them old Injun legends. Just tales, boy. Them ol' Utes had nothing better to do than sit around their fires at night an' tell each other stories. Ain't no such things as ghosts an' demons.' He shook his grey-flashed hair and laughter danced in his eyes. 'Why, if'n they fell off a hoss they'd blame it on a ghost or demon or bad spirit.' He shook his head as he poured himself a cup of coffee.

6

The boy smiled, a nervous, twitchy smile, not entirely convinced. Jimmy Tolliver, a boy at school, had told him that a giant snake lived up on Hollow Mountain. The Indians said that that was the reason for all the caves and tunnels. It was where the snake lived and it slithered around inside the mountain waiting to eat unsuspecting folk. Thinking of the story now made the boy shudder and he shut it from his mind.

The sound was like no other he had ever heard before and it woke him up. Somehow he had managed to fall asleep. Outside the storm still rolled about the mountain but its former fury had abated somewhat. The time between the lightning flashes and the thunder had grown longer. He sat up, pulling the blanket around his shoulders, and listened.

Above the sound of the fading storm he heard a low hiss and accompanying it a strange, grating rasp. It seemed to be coming from the area of the shaft at the rear of the cave.

The fire had shrunk to a mound of red, glowing embers and dark shadows pressed in from all directions. His pa remained in undisturbed slumber. Silently the boy rose and with the blanket still clasped about his shoulders moved to the edge of the barely visible shaft opening and stood there, listening.

The sound was growing louder, more urgent, more insistent and became mixed with tiny squealing cries that froze his blood. Something was coming up the shaft and with it came a coldness.

The boy ran back and woke his pa and then

together they stood at the shaft listening.

'What is it, Pa?'

'Ain't never heard the like afore,' the man admitted. He went back to the glowing embers of the fire, picked up a length of dry branch from the floor and thrust it into the ashes. It took only a few minutes for it to catch fire and then the man returned to the shaft with it clasped in one hand.

'You get back by the fire, boy,' he instructed and when the boy had moved back, he hunkered down at the edge of the shaft, holding the flaming brand out over it.

'Careful, Pa,' the boy begged.

The mysterious sounds had greatly increased by now. The man peered down, moving the flaming branch back and forth, setting up dancing shadows that scampered silently around him.

'Reckon it's jus' echoes. Water moving mebbe in tunnels deeper in the mountain,' the man called back doubtfully, then he gave a startled cry and fell back on to the seat of his pants. The makeshift torch flew from his hand and rolled against the wall, the flame flickering madly.

What happened next was quick and terrifying. The man had turned himself on to hands and knees facing away from the shaft and was in the act of climbing to his feet when something reared up out of the shaft. In the flickering, spluttering light that flared and dimmed the terrified boy glimpsed a giant grey head with huge, grey, blind eyes above a crooked mouth tipped with large, broken fangs rear up over his pa. He cried out in terror.

'Get out, boy, get out afore it's too late,' the man hollered.

'Pa!' the boy screamed.

'Run, boy, run!' the man yelled, panic in his voice as the huge, grey, glistening creature, hissing and roaring, for that's how it seemed to the petrified youngster, lunged at the man and drove him down on his face.

The torch flickered out, plunging the boy into heart-stopping darkness. The horse and pony stamped their hoofs, whinnying in the terror that the man's voice had conveyed to them.

'Pa!' the boy yelled into the slurping, gurgling darkness and in that instant a brief flicker of lightning lit up the cave. For one terrifying instant the boy looked into the mouth of hell. His pa was no more to be seen, lost amid writhing, serpentine coils. With a yell of fear the boy's courage left him. He turned and ran from the cave entrance and out into the rain lashed darkness.

'The gold's cursed, everyone knows it, but they still go a-looking fer it.' The old man smiled as he raised dark eyes in a weather-seamed face to the group of young men bellied up to the bar. They turned their heads to stare at him. He leaned back in his seat and lifted his glass, squinting through the amber liquid before lowering it and fixing his gaze on the youngsters. Sunlight patterned the dusty floor of the saloon around him. 'Trouble is, they don' ever come back; leastways not alive.' He tossed the contents of the glass down his throat before banging it down on to the scarred and pitted surface of the table before him.

Tobe Kellman turned his back on the bar and rested on his elbows, a smile on his lean, handsome, face. Hair the colour of corn in the bright morning sun waved back across his head and fell about his ears.

'How's that, old man?' Tobe threw his two companions a quick amused glance before looking with blue, smiling eyes at the old man.

Cajun Bokes returned the youngsters' stare with a sour grimace.

'Seen 'em come, but they don' stay long; jus' long enough to die. That's what happens to anyone who goes a-looking for Brogan's gold,' Cajun said.

'Ain't polite to listen to a private conversation, old man.' Frank Tooley, standing to the right of Kellman spoke up. A head shorter than Tobe Kellman's six foot three inches he peered across at Cajun with dark eyes in a square-jawed, aggressive face topped with dark, curly hair. What he lacked in height he made up for in his stocky build.

'Couldn't help overhearing being as you jawed so loudly,' Cajun replied.

'You saying we got big mouths, mister?' The last of the trio, Mort Simmons, lank hair spilling down over his ears glared a challenge at Cajun. He was the same height as Tooley, but thin and wiry. They were all dressed in range clothes dusty from travel.

'Mebbe I got big ears?' Cajun countered.

Tobe Kellman's face split into a wide, attractive grin and before Mort could frame an answer he said:

10

'Figure you for being the one they call Cajun Bokes.'
Tobe straightened up, turned, fisted the bottle and
headed towards Cajun. He stopped in front of the
table and extended the bottle to fill the old man's
glass but Cajun covered it with a big, calloused hand.

'Why you asking?' Eyes full of suspicion settled on
Tobe's smiling face, never leaving it as Tooley and
Simmons sidled up and joined Tobe. Cajun's sharp
eyes had quickly noticed that they all wore their guns
at waist-level. He figured them for cowhands.

'Heard it said that there was but one man in
Willow Creek who could tell a body 'bout Brogan's
gold an' that must be you. I'm Tobe Kellman and
these two are Frank Tooley an' Mort Simmons. Be
obliged you take a drink wi' us, Mr Bokes.'

Cajun's face split into a thin, derisive smile. 'That's
my daddy's name, son. Folks jus' call me Cajun.' He
removed his hand from the top of his glass and
leaned back. 'Sure, why not? Be real unsociable to
turn down a drink from such fine-looking boys. Take
a seat, boys an' we'll mebbe jaw a spell.'

'You said the gold's cursed?' Tobe Kellman
prompted after they were all seated and Cajun's glass
was full.

'Cursed to hell an' back an' then some,' Cajun
said, nodding his grizzled head before running a
thick-fingered hand through a tough mane of iron-
grey hair.

'How'd you mean, cursed?' Mort Simmons questioned, an earnest look on his thin, lank-haired
features.

'Blood, boy. It's got the curse o' blood on it,'

11

Cajun said dramatically. 'Twelve men rode with that gold the day Carl Brogan took it, an' twelve men died. Five men rode wi' Brogan, but he didn't wanna split that gold up an' get just a sixth share; he wanted it all, so he killed the five who rode wi' him an' I guess it killed Brogan in the end 'cause he wus never heard o' again. He an' the gold took to the mountains an' that was the last seen o' him. That makes a total of eighteen men.' Cajun shook his head dolefully.

'Mebbe he made it across the mountains,' Frank Tooley suggested. 'Him an' the gold are back East living high, off the hog. Or mebbe west, California or south to Mexico . . . .'

'Mebbe Chinee or Africa,' Cajun cut in with a grin and shook his head. 'Boy, you'd have ol' Brogan all over the world if'n you had it your way.'

'So how come you're so sure he didn't make it off the mountain?' Tobe raised his eyebrows.

Cajun snorted. 'One man on his own wi' all that gold an' men out searching for him. Brogan's ugly mug was known to all the searchers, but, like I said afore, he was never seen again. Hollow Mountain took him, right enough, him an' the gold.' Cajun nodded, then fixed them with a piercing gaze. 'It's a strange place for sure up there. The Utes have a name for it that translates as Land o' the Bad Spirits. Them Injuns keep away from it, an' that goes for you boys too. Go home an' grow old, boys. The only thing you'll get on the mountain is dead.'

The three exchanged smiling glances.

12

'Don' reckon no Injun spirits are gonna keep us from looking for the gold.' Tobe spoke up and the others nodded, but Cajun did not smile, just shook his head sadly.

'The gold's cursed to hell an' back, boy. It's got the taste o' blood in its shiny, yellow soul an' it wants more. An' it gets more 'cause o' the fools that go a-looking for it. They never come back.'

'You calling us fools, mister?' Frank Tooley eyed Cajun, eyes sparking belligerently.

Cajun's face cracked in a grin. 'Kinda feisty, ain't you, son? Don' mind me. I speak as I see an' I'll say it agin. Anyone who goes a-looking for Brogan's gold has got a little o' the fool in him.'

'How come you ain't looked for the gold?' Tobe asked.

'Got my own silver-mine up there, son. Keeps me in whiskey an' beans so I ain't complainin'.'

'An' the spirits don't bother you?' Mort Simmons wanted to know.

'Why should they, son? I ain't looking for Brogan's gold. It belongs to them an' the mountain now an' they got their own ways to keep it hidden, an' their own ways to deal wi' those who come a-looking for it.' He nodded meaningfully.

'Well, ain't no spirits gonna stop us,' Frank Tooley sneered, 'nor no fool stories.'

Cajun shrugged. 'You asked, I told.'

A shadow fell across the table and the three looked up to find the blocky form of Sheriff Clance Folley standing there, badge gleaming on his tan vest.

13

'Howdy, Cajun,' he greeted, a smile spreading his thickly mustachioed lips.

'Sheriff,' Cajun returned.

'See you got yoursel' some new friends. Ain't seen you boys around here afore.' He moved to Cajun's side, hooked his thumbs behind the buckle of his gunbelt and stared down at the three from eyes shadowed by his hat brim. Light from the window at his back surrounded him, in halo.

'Ain't been here afore, Sheriff,' Tobe replied brightly.

Cajun gave a snorting laugh. 'They come a-looking for Brogan's gold. I told 'em to go home. It ain't worth it.'

The sheriff nodded. 'Reckon Cajun's right on that. Happen you should take his advice.'

'Ain't no law says we can't look for Brogan's gold is there, Sheriff?' Frank Tooley spoke up.

The sheriff laughed. 'Hell no, son. If'n a body wants to go up into the mountains an' get his'sel killed, that's his affair.'

'That's good, 'cause that's where we 'uns is headed,' Frank said stubbornly.

The sheriff studied the other's set face and then gave a shrug of his shoulders. 'I can see you boys have made up your minds, but take it from me, an' I've seen a lot like you, wi' that same eager-for-gold look in their eyes, forget it. A fella's gotta be crazy to go up there. Now ol' Cajun here, well, he's allus been crazy, so he don' count. Ain't that right, Cajun?'

'That's surely a fact, Sheriff,' Cajun agreed with a chuckle.

'Well, you've done your duty, Sheriff, an' we 'uns are obliged for your advice, but we can take care o' oursels,' Tobe said. Frank Tooley and Mort Simmons nodded in agreement.

The sheriff studied them thoughtfully for a second or two, then shrugged his lips. 'Then good luck to you, boys.'

'We'll be back, Sheriff,' Tobe said.

'Sure hope so, son, sure hope so,' the sheriff murmured.

The following morning, the three, provisions loaded on to two pack-mules, rode up into the mountains above Willow Creek and were never seen again.

Willow Creek lay amid the foothills of the San Juan Mountains in Colorado, fed by a tributary from the Animas river which tumbled down from Silverton to Durango. Summer had all but gone and autumn cloaked the slopes around Willow Creek with drifts of purple aster and sprays of yellow-flowered rabbit-brush set before a backdrop of willow groves. Higher up scrub oak and aspen took over and in their turn became the smoky green of blue spruce, ponderosa and limber pine before the cold, grey, granite peaks, tipped with white, soared against the deep blue of the sky.

A warm breeze, still warm from the lingering summer days, blew along main street, stirring dust around the straggle of clapboard buildings. Sheriff Clance Folley, on his first cup of coffee of the day, glanced up from his desk as the outer door opened and a girl entered. She was clad in pants and boots and a blue check shirt beneath a hide jacket. The sheriff wasn't sure it was a female until she swept her hat off and released a cascade of gleaming, blonde hair.

He stared at her with a sort of amused fascination as she approached him and came to a halt before the desk; ladies dressed as men were not a common sight in Willow Creek and beneath the mannish rig was a mighty fine-looking woman. She loosened her coat and the shirt did little to hide the generous curves of her body.

'Howdy, ma'am. You look like you've travelled a-ways. Take a seat.' He waved a hand towards a high-backed wooden chair. She dropped into it and fixed him with a pair of wide, blue eyes.

'Kansas City, Sheriff.'

'That's a-ways,' he agreed. 'So what brings a Kansas City gal to Willow Creek?'

'I'm looking for my brother, Tobe Kellman, I'm Sara Kellman. He came here with two of his friends, Mort Simmons and Frank Tooley some three, nearly four months ago and they've not been seen since.'

The sheriff eyed her and placed his cup down. 'I'm forgetting my manners, ma'am. Can I get you a coffee? Got a clean cup an' the coffee's fresh made this morning, an' you look like you could stand a cup 'bout now.'

She gave a wan smile. 'I think I could,' she agreed. 'Been on the trail a long while.' She relaxed back into the chair as the sheriff busied himself with a coffee-pot that stood on top of a pot-belly stove.

'So what makes you think your brother an' his

friends are here, ma'am?' he asked after handing her the coffee and settling himself back in his seat. She took an appreciative sip of the hot, bitter brew before answering.

'He an' his friends had this fool idea of looking for some lost gold. Rogan's, Bogan's . . .'

'Brogan's gold, ma'am,' Sheriff Folley corrected and she nodded.

'They heard about it from some fella in a saloon in Kansas City an' reckoned it was better'n working for a living.' There was a bitter note to her words. 'I told Tobe it was a fool idea, but he got it into his head that he could find the missing gold an' Simmons an' Tooley went along wi' him.'

The sheriff grunted, shook his head and pulled a face in thought. 'Mind there were some eager-looking fella's here a-ways back,' he nodded. 'Could'a been them.'

'Then they're here?' she prompted eagerly.

'Here an' gone ma'am,' he said and her face fell. 'People come here all the time looking for that gold. No one's ever found it, that's if'n it's even there. I 'member now. They was a-talking to ol' Cajun when I happened up. We both told them it was a dam' fool thing to do. It ain't safe up there, even for a mountain man. Three city boys . . . .' He shook his head negatively.

'Cajun?' She prompted.

'Yes, ma'am. Cajun Bokes, he's got himsel' a silver-mine up in the mountains. Comes into town once in a while, though I ain't seen him for a spell now.'

'Do you think he'll know more about them?' Hope

17

sprang in her eyes. The sheriff sniffed and pulled a
face.

'Cajun keeps to hissel'. He ain't, what you call, a
mixing man.'

'Can I talk to him? He might know something.'

'Like I say, ol' Cajun, he don't come to town
much.'

'Well, where can I find him?'

'That'd be a mite difficult, ma'am. Cajun's mine is
a two-day ride up into the mountains. Ain't no fancy
streets up there, an' unless you know the way, ain't
easy to find. A body could get lost up there, real easy.
Maybe your brother an' his friends are still up there.
If'n so, the weather'll be changing in a few weeks an'
if'n they ain't down by the time the snows come . . . .'
He spread his arms in a shrug, leaving the rest
unsaid. 'I'm sorry, ma'am.'

'Can't you organize a search party, Sheriff?'

'Sorry, ma'am. You won't find a body willing to go
up there. It's a bad place. If'n I was you I'd head on
back to Kansas City and wait a spell longer. Could be
they're on their way home right now. Mebbe they've
come off the mountain by another way an' headed
for Durango to find work. Perhaps feeling a little
foolish at not finding the gold.'

'Or they could be dead,' she added dully, a sparkle
of tears in her eyes that she bravely fought back.

'Or they could be dead,' the sheriff agreed slowly.
'It's happened afore an' I reckon it'll happen agin.
Folks come here looking for that gold an' are never
seen agin. Cajun says the gold's cursed. The mountain took it an' it ain't giving it back. Hollow

18

Mountain: the place of bad spirits. Go home ma'am.'

She shook her head defiantly. 'I can't, Sheriff. Tobe is the only family I have left. If you won't help me then I'll find someone who will.'

'Not in Willow Creek, ma'am.'

'Then I'll go alone.'

The sheriff sighed. 'Short of locking you up until you see sense, ma'am, I can't stop you, but you'll be wise to keep away from the mountain. Grown men get into trouble up there.'

'I'm tougher than I look,' she snapped back. 'I can look after myself.'

'Mebbe, but men who know mountains die up there.'

'I'll take my chance, Sheriff. Thank you for the coffee.' She rose to her feet and he watched her march, stiff-backed, out of the office and shook his head.

CHAPTER 2

The horse snorted. There was fire in its eyes and temper in its laid-back ears as it faced the two men in the corral that held it prisoner. It was a beautiful, raindrop Appaloosa stallion, its white body dappled with brownish/black pear-shaped markings which resembled large rainspots, thus giving it its name. It rose up on its hindquarters and pawed the air, defying the men to come closer. In the corral next to it a dozen mares and colts bunched together, whinnying nervously.

Dusk Landers, clad only in a pair of Levis and boots eyed the animal warily. Somewhere in his mid-twenties, he was a tall, handsome man. Dark hair spilled from beneath a low-crowned, tan Stetson. Beard-stubble decorated his lower face and a smile tugged at his lips. The smile was reflected in eyes shaded by the brim of the Stetson.

Sweat dappled his muscular, sun-bronzed torso. In his hands he held a lasso, ready to toss over the Appaloosa's head. The second man, Joe Little Wolf was a full-blooded Ute who could have been any age from fifty to eighty: it was hard to determine from his passive, creased, olive-skinned face in which brown eyes sparkled and shone with life. His iron-grey hair was pulled back tight over his scalp and tied in a single ponytail which reached down to his shoulder blades. He was taller and broader than Dusk, his powerful body encased in buckskin pants and shirt, moccasins on his feet.

'Come on, Joe, you're moving like an old man,' Dusk called out and Joe eyed him.

'I am an old man,' Joe rumbled back haughtily and Dusk laughed as he stepped towards the skittish Appaloosa.

Joe looked beyond the younger man. 'Rider coming in,' he sang out. Dusk stepped back from the horse and cast a look over his shoulder at the distant rider.

'Anyone we know?'

'Woman wearing white man's clothes,' Joe said.

Dusk raised questioning eyebrows and turned to face the approaching rider, moving towards the corral fence as she came nearer. He laid aside the rope and reached for his shirt, pulling it on as she reined to a halt. With a quick, fluid movement he scaled the corral fence and dropped lightly to the ground on the other side.

Sara Kellman stared over him at the Appaloosa, admiration in her blue eyes. 'He's a beautiful animal,' she said.

'Thank you. It's been a long time since a pretty squaw has called me that.' Joe spoke up, his dead-pan face giving nothing away, but his eyes sparkled with amusement. He had followed Dusk and now stood a little to one side with the corral fence between them.

Sara, startled by the unexpected reply, coloured. Dusk found it hard to suppress a smile.

'How can we help you, ma'am?' Dusk asked as he buttoned his shirt.

'I . . . I'm looking for Dusk Landers.'

'Well you've found him, ma'am, an' this 'ere's Joe Little Wolf.' Dusk jerked a thumb in Joe's direction.

'Wise man of the Ute nation,' Joe informed solemnly, with the same twinkle in his eye.

Dusk sighed. 'You'll have to forgive Joe, ma'am. He tends to get a bit gabby when we have visitors. Now why would you be looking for me?'

'I'll come straight to the point, Mr Landers . . . .'

'Call me Dusk, ma'am.'

'Mr Landers,' she persisted primly. I need a guide to take me up into the mountains. You were recommended. I am willing to pay twenty dollars for your service.'

Dusk looked up at her thoughtfully and she sensed a change in both men. Joe Little Wolf regarded her now with cold fathomless eyes.

Dusk massaged the back of his neck with a hand and squinted up at her. 'Now why would you be wanting to go up there, ma'am?' he asked quietly.

'I'm looking for my brother and his friends; they disappeared on the mountain a while back. I have reason to believe, hope, that a man called Cajun Bokes might have some knowledge as to their whereabouts. I need a guide to take me to him.'

'Cajun Bokes,' Dusk repeated softly.

23

'You know of him?'

'Ain't many that don't in these parts.'

'Then you'll take me to him?' Hope sprang in her voice.

'Sorry, m'am. My advice to you is to stay off the mountain.'

'I can perhaps stretch to thirty dollars.'

'It ain't the money, ma'am,' Dusk interrupted abruptly. 'The mountain's no place for a woman.'

Fire flared in her eyes. 'So everyone tells me,' she snapped back. 'I guess this woman will have to rely on herself to get things done.'

'The mountain kills folks, ma'am. It has done for more years than I've been around. If'n it's taken your brother an' his friends, chances are you'll never find their bodies, an' like as not it'll take you.'

'That's a chance I'll just have to take, Mr Landers, on my own. I'm sorry to have troubled you.' She dragged her mount's head around and dug her booted heels into its ribs.

'Dying's bad enough, ma'am. On your own it's pure hell,' Dusk called out after her. If she heard his dire call she did not acknowledge it. 'Damn' fool woman,' he growled under his breath.

'A woman of spirit,' Joe said approvingly.

Dusk looked up broodingly at the flank of the mountain that reared to the west of the deep valley. It brought back dark memories that he would rather not dwell on. Joe saw the sadness creep into the other's eyes: a sadness that could draw the youngster into a cocoon of melancholia that could last for days, unless he could pull him back before

24

he plunged over the brink.

'A fine woman. Make a man happy between the blankets,' Joe said wickedly and waited for a reaction from Dusk.

Dusk tore his eyes from the mountain and settled them on the old Indian. 'A man o' your age should-n't be thinking o' such things.'

A smile crossed Joe's face. 'When you get to my age, thinking 'bout it is all you have left,' he replied and breathed a sigh of relief when a smile broke across Dusk's handsome features.

'I don't know who's worst to be around. A feisty woman or a crazy ol' Indian,' he commented. 'Come on, let's go an' sort that horse out,' he added with a chuckle.

Joe glanced up at the mountain as Dusk removed his shirt and scaled the corral fence. One day the boy would have to face his fears, lay the ghosts of the past, and maybe that day was not far off, but until then . . . .

As the two set to work the fickle hand of fate prepared to declare its bid, for that day had arrived.

The following morning the two hitched up the buck-board and with Joe at the reins, drove into Willow Creek. There were supplies to be got and prepara-tions made before the arrival of the winter snows. It was true that the snows were many weeks away yet and riding through the warm, autumn morning between high banks of goldenrod and purple aster glowing in the sunlight, it was hard to think of the harsh, bleak days ahead.

Willow Creek bustled as they rode in on the buckboard, its iron-bound wheels bouncing in the hard, rutted road. Joe reined the pair of horses pulling the buckboard to a halt outside the general store.

The round face of Homer Billings, owner of the store, lit up as the two entered and he came out from behind his counter. He was short and paunchy and wrapped, as always, in his white, protective apron.

'Howdy Dusk, Joe. Ain't seen you boys in a while.'

'Busy times, Homer, busy times,' Dusk sang out, his nose twitching. The general store had a special smell all of its own. The smell of leather, herbs for cooking. The scent from the jars of boiled sweets, cinnamon, coffee. The smells mingled and merged until they became unique and wonderful. 'Got me a whole list o' needs that I hope you can fill, Homer.' Dusk passed a list to the store owner. Homer's eyes darted down the page.

'Reckon I can supply all o' these,' Homer said with a nod. 'Why don' you boys grab a cup o' Martha's coffee an' they'll be ready when you've finished. Cakes are good today an' there's some real nice apple-and-cinnamon pie.

'Sounds good. 'Preciate it, Homer,' Dusk said with a laugh.

Martha, Homer's wife, ran a small coffee parlour in the back of the store and always had a good selection of cakes and pies to go with the coffee.

As the two made their way down narrow aisles between tall shelf-units cluttered with all manner of dry goods, Sophie Billings appeared in front of Dusk. She was a bubbly blonde girl with a generous figure and an even more generous nature.

'I heard you tell Pa that you had needs to fill, Dusk. Do I come on that list?' she asked coyly.

'Sophie Billings. What could you be meaning by that?' Dusk demanded with a smile on his face. For an answer Sophie stood on tiptoe and whispered something in his ear. She ended it with a giggle and darted away, leaving Dusk standing there speechless with a crimson face.

Joe eyed the younger man with amused eyes. 'White man turn to redman,' he commented drily.

'It's . . . it's hot in here,' Dusk replied weakly. Later, after a good filling of coffee and pie, Dusk and Joe returned to the front of the store where Homer had piled the list of stores on the broad counter. Joe eyed Homer.

'You think Dusk look more like redman than me?'

Homer peered intently up at Dusk. 'Does look a little flushed. You feeling OK, Dusk? Could be going down wi' something.'

'More like something coming up,' Joe countered with a look at Dusk, and Dusk's face reddened again. While the old Indian maintained an impassive face, his eyes were alight with laughter.

It was then that Sophie appeared again and turned his world into a nightmare of concealed embarrass-ment. 'Something up, Dusk?' she asked innocently and even Joe's face cracked a little.

'Gotta get these loaded,' Dusk said in a strangled voice, grabbing up a heavy sack of flour and stagger-ing towards the door with it.

'Well, you take care, Dusk. That's a mite heavy. You

27

make sure you don' pull something.'

'I won't, Homer,' Dusk said as he headed for the door. The door was only partly open and with his hands full Dusk had to pause and hook a foot around it to open it wider.

'Here, let me hold it for you, Dusk,' Sophie called out darting across to hold the door open for him.

Homer grimaced at Dusk's bent-double posture. 'That boy's asking for back trouble carrying it like that. Take care o' that back, Dusk.' Homer raised his voice. 'If'n you feel any stiffness come an' see Sophie. We got some new potions in from the East.' By the time Homer had said the last sentence Dusk had already disappeared through the door.

Joe grabbed up a pile of items. 'Potions. I remember.'

At the door Sophie looked up at Joe with a wicked light in her eyes. 'That's right what Pa says. If'n Dusk feels any stiffness he's to come an' see me right away.'

'I make sure he knows,' Joe promised and grinned as he headed for the buckboard.

Dusk stood by the buckboard, back to the store, tears of laughter now streaming down his face. He glared at Joe as the other came up and deposited the items in the buckboard.

'Goddammit, Joe. Between you an' Sophie . . .' He shook his head and brushed the tears from his eyes and face. 'I'm sending you back to the reservation. You're fired.'

'I've never been hired,' Joe replied.

'Let's get the rest o' the stuff and pay Homer,' Dusk said, getting himself under control.

Back in the store they had to wait a few minutes while Homer served another customer.

'OK, gents, that'll be twenty-two dollars even.' As he took the money and deposited it in a cash box, he added, 'By the way, I hope you didn't mind, Dusk. There was a girl here looking for someone to take her up to Cajun's place. I gave her your name. Only them no-account Lacey boys, Coot and Beau, looked ready to take up her offer. I warned her off an' gave her your name. Girl alone wi' them two, makes a body shudder.' Homer gave a shudder to emphasize his words.

'Yeh, she came by, but I turned her down. Told her to go home.'

'Figured you might. Reckon everyone in town has told her the same. I remember the three boys. Came in for supplies. Real excited. I told them at the time to give up the idea o' looking for Brogan's gold, but they never paid heed. No one ever does,' he ended sadly. 'She wouldn't either, more's the pity.'

Dusk's brow furrowed as he eyed Homer. 'How do you mean, she wouldn't either?'

'She's gone up on the mountain on her own. Came in early this morning, bought a week's supplies an' lit out o' here. Happen she'll see sense afore too long though an' turn back.' He pulled a face. 'Then mebbe not,' he shrugged. 'She seemed real determined.'

'Thanks, Homer.' Dusk turned abruptly and headed for the door. Joe picked up the last of the supplies and followed him.

'See you boys agin soon. Take care now,' Homer called out.

29

Dusk was already in the seat of the buckboard as Joe climbed up and took up the reins. Dusk said nothing as they rattled out of town. He sat there in silent, brooding thought until they began the descent into the valley with the cabin, corrals and barns in view below them.

'She'll get her fool self killed,' Dusk opined, breaking the silence at last.

'We make our own destiny,' Joe replied sombrely. 'Sometimes good, sometimes bad.'

'Well, this is one o' the bad ones for her,' Dusk snapped back. 'Could be the last one she'll ever make.'

'That is the way of destiny,' Joe replied enigmatically.

'That's Indian foolishness. What are you saying: that once a person sets out to do something there's no going back? That's it? Even if'n they are staring death in the face they jus' go blindly on? I don' buy that, Joe.'

'Destiny is in the eye of he who seeks. He sees the end not as others see his end. The girl sees only of finding her lost brother. She refuses to see him as dead and that blinds her to her own danger, which others see and she does not.' That was a long speech for Joe. 'Her destiny can be changed, but only by another changing it for her.' Joe brought the buckboard to a halt in front of the cabin and Dusk jumped down and vanished silently, morosely, in the direction of the twin corrals.

Joe clambered down and unloaded the buckboard. The boy had finally reached the moment of his own destiny. What he decided now would shape

30

the rest of his life. The wrong decision could make or destroy him and there was nothing he, Joe, could do to help him make that decision. As he unhitched the horses from the buckboard Joe saw Dusk, riding a horse bareback, heading east.

It was noon before Dusk reappeared. Joe had the rainbow Appaloosa roped on a long tether and was letting it canter around the corral. Dusk rode up to the corral and slid from the horse. Joe shortened the tether and let the Appaloosa come up to him. The animal was calmer now. Joe had a way with horses. He slipped the rope from the horse and walked towards where Dusk was standing.

'I think we have an understanding,' Joe said, nodding towards the Appaloosa, noting the brooding look still in the boy's eyes, but with it something else.

'I'm going after her, Joe. I can't let her die up there.' A smile touched his lips. 'I guess I've got to give her destiny a prod in the right direction.'

'We go together,' Joe said promptly.

'I thought you might say that. I stopped off at Cal Greeley's spread an' he's gonna send a couple o' hands over to look after the horses 'til we get back.'

Joe nodded as he climbed over the corral fence and dropped down before Dusk.

'Makes me wonder why we put a gate in. We never use it,' Joe commented.

'Thanks, Joe.' Dusk held out a hand. 'I hope I didn't offend you back there calling your beliefs foolish?'

Joe ignored the hand. Instead he stepped forward

31

and grabbed Dusk in a bear hug.

'Why not? It is foolish,' Joe responded lightly.

CHAPTER 3

When Sara Kellman rode out of Willow Creek earlier that morning, she did not go unobserved. From their tumbledown shack on the edge of town the Lacey brothers, Beau and Coot, watched her pass by. The two sat on ancient rockers on the crumbling veranda that fronted the shack, drinking whiskey, hidden by the shade thrown by the wooden overhang above and the riot of tangled shrubbery that fronted the property.

'Lookee at her go. Sashaying by like she's a-going on a picnic,' Coot sang out.

'Picnic needs bodies for company. Reckon she needs company,' Beau added as he passed the bottle across to Coot.

The brothers were as alike as two peas in a pod. Thin, scrawny men in their mid-forties with lank, greasy hair and dirty, matted beards. The exposed flesh on their thin faces was grimy with dirt, eyes sunk in deep, dirty sockets. They looked alike and dressed alike, in shabby, old black suits and stained blue shirts. The only way to tell them apart was that

Beau had a scar on his left cheek which ran from the outer corner of his eye passing under his bony nose to disappear into his moustache.

They managed to scrape through life existing on menial jobs about town. Swamping out the two saloons, clearing out the livery stable and just about any dirty job that folks didn't want to do. The jobs kept them in food and whiskey, just, but they were always on the look-out for easy money and the girl represented that. Beau had already worked out in his mind what the horse and saddle would be worth and knew a place on the county line that would take both with no questions asked.

'Reckon she got money?' Coot asked, passing the bottle back.

'Reckon we 'uns can soon find that out,' Beau replied with, a nasty laugh.

'Doggone it, Beau, we mighter struck gold wi' that little filly. Get us a decent bottle o' whiskey. When we gonna do it?'

'Plenty o' time yet, brother Coot; let her get well away from town.'

'We don' wanna lose her in the mmountains,' Coot pointed out anxiously.

'Ain't likely to happen, brother. Ain't but one trail to follow up that mountain an' takes nigh on two days afore it runs out. By that time we'll have introduced oursel's.'

'Scoot, Beau, we can have oursel's a real good time.' Coot's eyes shone at the prospect.

'We'll ride out later, catch up wi' her afore nightfall an' have us a little party. Then tomorrow ride over to Fat Jake's to do a little selling. Happen Jake's got some o' that special whiskey. Mebbe get us a couple o' bottles an' still have money to jingle.' Beau stretched his thin legs out contentedly.

'Hell, Beau, I don't know as I can wait that long,' Coot moaned, gripping his hands together in his lap.

'Gotta be patient, brother. Here, take another pull o' this.' He passed the bottle back to Coot who took it eagerly. He raised it to his mouth, but paused, lowering it again.

'Ain't no chance of anyone going there to look for her is there? I mean later?'

'Relax, brother, relax. I heard she was on her own. No family 'cepting that brother she's gone a-looking for an' he's most likely dead. Folks warned her not to go up there so ain't no one gonna be surprised when she don' come back an' ain't no one gonna be looking for her, ever, an' even if'n they did, they'll never find her. Times are looking good, brother, times are looking good.'

'Hot damn! I'll drink to that,' Coot cried out joyously.

Unaware of the danger she was in, Sara relaxed as she followed the trail up through the groves of willow, enjoying the calm serene beauty that surrounded her. Now that she had started her anxiety evaporated away. The trail was wide and easy to follow and she felt that it would be no problem finding the elusive Cajun Bokes.

The trail continued up, past clumps of clematis hanging from the trees with their white plumes of feathery seed-heads forming tattered curtains. By noon the willow forest had given way to stands of scrub oak and aspen with the occasional lodgepole pine rearing high into the sky. With the thinning of the trees she was afforded breathtaking panoramic views of vast cliffs sweeping down into tree-filled valleys far below and the soaring peaks of the San Juans. And once, between two high pinnacles, she caught a glimpse of the rugged, snowcapped Rockies marching north.

By mid-afternoon the mountains had closed around her, hemming her in, and a gorge had opened up on one side of the trail, its sheer sides dropping down to a meandering river far below which tumbled and cascaded over fallen rocks. Eventually, in a tree-ringed clearing, she slid stiffly from the horse and eased the kinks from her back. Birds chattered in the trees and insects hummed around her. In a few hours it would be nightfall; she could have continued on for a spell longer, but decided she had done enough for one day and set about making camp for the coming night.

There was a small, tinkling stream which emerged from the rocks and tree-roots on the far side of the clearing and tumbled into a pool. The water was fresh and icy cold, but very welcome. After unsaddling the horse and tending to its needs she made a small fire and settled a coffee-pot on it. Everything was just perfect.

'Coffee sure smells good,' a grating voice said and her perfect world was about to turn into a nightmare. She jumped to her feet as Coot and Beau Lacey, leading their horses, entered the clearing. Her heart thundered in her breast at their sudden appearance.

'Sure could do wi' some o' that, Beau,' Coot Lacey agreed, grinning through his beard, eyes fixed on her heaving chest. 'Yup, sure could do wi' some o' that,' he repeated softly.

Sara did her best to hide the sudden pulse of fear that gripped her.

'Who are you and what do you want?' she demanded. Her rifle was with the saddle boot and out of reach.

'Now is that any way to greet a fella traveller, girl?' Beau goaded. 'Mighty lonely up here. Figure a body might need some friendly company. Wouldn't you figure that too, brother?' Beau's eyes were fixed on her: small, hard eyes that offered anything but friendship.

'Be real unneighbourly to turn away folks wi' night coming on, an' all,' Coot added. By now both men had dropped the reins of their mounts and were circling the fire, approaching her from both sides.

Fear congealed in her eyes. She had backed as far as she could and now she was trapped.

'I saw you in Willow Creek,' she said faintly.

'That you did,' Beau agreed. 'I'm Beau and this 'ere's Coot an' we're real pleased to meet you. Ain't that so, brother?'

'Too damn right.' Coot nodded his head vigorously.

'Take the coffee, just leave me alone,' she cried out.

'Oh, we inten' to, girl, that an' a sight more,' Beau

37

said softly and chuckled. He made a sudden move towards her. She turned protectively to face him, forgetting Coot for an instant. By the time she remembered him it was too late.

Hands, thin and hurtful, grabbed her upper arms from behind and with a snort Coot pulled her back against his body.

'I got her, Beau, I got her,' Coot sang out gleefully.

She screamed and struggled, but Coot's hands were like iron bands about her arms, squeezing the flesh in a tight, unbreakable grip through the thin material of the shirt; she had removed her coat earlier.

Beau came forward, grinning evilly. 'Reckon it's time you showed us what you got, girl.' His hands closed over her breasts, kneading and squeezing.

Sara closed her eyes and screamed again, a high, despairing sound that sent birds squawking from the trees. The hands dropped away from her body.

'Shut it, girl!' Beau shouted and at the same time slapped her hard across the face. It caught her on the side of the mouth; she felt her lip split and tasted blood, but she stopped screaming. 'That sure is better,' Beau hissed and settled his hands back on her breasts.

'Let me have some o' that, Beau, let me have some,' Coot begged.

'You wait your turn, brother. Got me something to show the girl.' He smirked and his hands went to the buckle of his belt.

Anger surged through her, temporarily smothering the fear she felt. In a move that neither of the men expected, she brought her knee up hard between Beau's legs. Beau's grin turned to a mask of agony. Rancid breath whooshed over her from lips formed into an 'O' of pain. He grabbed at his injured parts, bending double as his legs buckled and he went to his knees, moaning.

'Hell, Beau, I don' reckon you'll be showing her anything,' Coot said with a laugh. 'Reckon I git first bite o' the apple.' But Coot's brag was short-lived as Sara raised a booted heel and brought it down hard on the instep of his left foot. She heard bones crunch followed by a keening scream of pain. And then she was free. She whirled and raked her hand across Coot's left cheek, her nails cutting three furrows in the flesh. Coot hopped away and dropped to the ground, clutching at his foot and then his face.

'She hurt me, the bitch hurt me. Bruk my goddamn foot and ripped my face open,' Coot shrieked out. Beau, eyes streaming with tears of pain, settled back on his calves and clawed a Colt Pioneer from a holster.

'She bruk my goddam balls,' Beau shouted back and wiped his eyes with his free hand to clear his tear-blurred vision. 'I'll put a goddamn bullet in her hide,' he added vengefully. For an instant he caught a glimpse of her disappearing over the bank of the clearing. He fired, but she was gone.

'Did you get her? Did you get the she-bitch?' Coot cried out.

'Done got away. But I'll git her an' she'll be real sorry,' Beau vowed.

Escape was the only thought in Sara's mind. To get

away from the two men at all costs, now. Beyond the clearing, she fled down a wooded slope. She had no real idea where she was going, but anywhere was better than the clearing. After using her knee on Beau and crushing Coot's foot, neither man would be in a position to move fast after her. Her only hope was to get away as far as possible and then try to make it back to Willow Creek on foot. It was a daunting prospect, but she had no other choice, so she stumbled blindly on, the sound of the shot giving her incentive. Night was coming and that would help to hide her from them.

She plunged through a thicket, thorns tearing her shirt and slicing the flesh beneath. She choked back a cry of agony, but could not suppress the scream of terror as the ground beneath her feet disappeared and she felt herself falling.

Joe Little Wolf crouched down on the mountain trail. He stared at the ground and then raised his eyes, following the trail up until it disappeared.

'Four horses, one moving light, three riders,' he said as he rose to his full height.

Still in the saddle, Dusk peered ahead. 'Our lady and her pack-horse. Sounds like she's got company.'

'Two tracks fresher than the first; one, two hours, mebbe three behind.'

'Unwelcome company,' Dusk mused. 'Someone's following her, mebbe planning a little surprise. She could be in trouble.' He sighed. 'For a lady whom no one wants to help she sure do attract attention.'

Joe swung astride his pinto and the two set off at a

faster pace. They had not been riding more than ten minutes when they heard the sound of a gunshot way off in the distance. The two reined to a halt, but there were no more shots. Grim-faced, they set off again.

Beau stood up painfully, hobbled awkwardly towards the groaning Coot and attempted to drag him to his feet.

'Mind my goddamn bruk foot,' Coot yelled.

'You'll git a bruk head if'n you don' git up,' Beau grated. 'I want that bitch. Now git up an' we'll git after her.'

'My face hurts,' Coot wailed miserably.

'You ain't walking on your face. We 'uns got some sorting out to do on accounts o' her. She's gonna pay for what she done.' There was a grim, vengeful note in Beau's voice.

Coot rose carefully to his feet, grimacing before hobbling gingerly around as Beau scrambled up the bank and paused at the top, looking back at him.

'You comin' or is you figuring on dancing the night away?'

'It's all right for you, you ain't got a bruk foot,' Coot moaned.

'If'n you don' get up here, brother, I'll put a bullet in your other foot an' that'll really give you something to moan 'bout.'

'Why are we 'uns running 'bout this goddamn mountain? Why not jus' take her horses an' stuff an' light outta here?'

' 'Cause I want her. Now get up here, brother, or

I'll put you in touch wi' ma an' pa. If'n you get my meaning?'

Coot blanched. Ma and Pa Lacey were long dead which made Beau's meaning real clear. He had never seen Beau so all-fired up before, except the time Beau had got his face cut by a whore over Denver way. He'd messed her up real bad, damn near cut her up into little pieces. The thought made him shudder. If the truth be known, Coot was a little scared of Beau and that made him forget his foot.

'Hold your horses, Beau, I'm a-coming,' Coot said miserably. As Coot scrambled up the bank and joined his brother they both heard the distant scream of fear. A smile crossed Beau's face.

'Happen she's run into a little trouble. Sure hope she ain't killed hersel . . . yet.'

Sara's eyes flickered open. She could see trees and an expanse of blue sky. The image wavered and then snapped back into focus. She tried to move and the effort forced a groan from her lips. She remembered falling and was now lying on her back looking up. A face came into view. Bearded, hostile, leering down at her. Another face joined the first.

'She's alive, Beau,' Coot sang out.

'Ain't that just fine an' dandy,' Beau replied. The two stood over the girl who lay helplessly at the bottom of a dried-up riverbed into which she had fallen. There were high, tree-lined banks on either side and the riverbed was strewn with water-smoothed boulders waiting for the autumn rains that would fill the deep gully with a roaring, foaming, torrent of water. In a way she had been lucky. She had fallen some twelve feet into a sandy pit between the boulders. A foot in any direction and she would most likely have broken her back on a boulder.

For a second Sara stared up at the faces; they were vaguely familiar, then her memory kicked in and everything came flooding back in dreadful, lurid detail, setting her heart pounding. She struggled to rise, but the movement sent waves of sickening pain from a dozen points around her body and she fell back helplessly.

Slowly Beau drew a knife. 'You hurt me, girl, an' for that you gotta pay.' He ran a hand over the scar on his cheek.

'She hurt me too, Beau, remember. Bruk my foot an' ripped my face,' Coot spoke up.

'I never did anything to you. Why are you doing this?' she cried out shrilly.

' 'Cause it's what we do,' Bleau replied.

'Don' kill her yet, Beau, not till I've had me a turn,' Coot said anxiously.

Mustering all her energy she rolled on to her side, scrambled on to hands and knees and climbed to her feet, the pain numbed by fear and a surge of adrenalin. She managed a few faltering steps before a wave of dizziness rolled over her. She turned and faced the two men defiantly, legs rubbery. The two watched her, amusement on their bearded faces.

'Ain't nowhere to run, girl,' Beau taunted. 'Reckon we'll let brother Coot here have 'is fun an' then I'll have mine.' He ran a grimy thumb along the blade of the knife and smiled.

Tears filled her eyes and rolled down her cheeks. She clenched her fists on her thighs as Coot, grinning from ear to ear, moved slowly towards her, his bad foot forgotten.

'Gonna have us some fun, girl, an' that's the pure truth o' it,' he cooed.

A feeling of utter hopelessness surged through her, but she refused to give in without a fight, no matter how much the odds were stacked against her. She rubbed the tears away and cast about for some means of defence. Her eyes fell on a length of tree-branch near her right foot. It was about two feet long, the bark stripped away and the wood beneath bone-white and baked hard by the sun. There were many such fragments littering the dry riverbed amid the boulders, washed down from the high valleys by the winter storms. She grabbed it up and faced the advancing Coot, determination in her face. It was not much of a weapon against two strong men, but it was all she had. If she had to die then she would die fighting.

CHAPTER 4

Coot stopped. 'We sure got a feisty one here, Beau,' he called out. 'Gonna be a real pleasure to tame this she-cat.' He eyed her and gently touched the seeping, bloody gouge-marks on his cheek. 'A real pleasure.' Now it was his turn to pull a knife. Grinning widely, wary eyes on the length of wood she clutched in both hands, he began to close the gap between them.

'Take one more step an' you're a dead man, Coot Lacey.' The grim voice accompanied the words with the sound of a gun hammer clicking back.

For a second time Coot stopped dead in his tracks, frozen to the spot, mouth dropping open, unable to believe his ears. He dropped the knife, then whirled around, pushing his hands to the sky, staring wide-eyed in the direction of the owner of the voice.

'I ain't reaching for no gun,' he wailed fearfully, his former bravado at only having to face an unarmed girl, deserting him.

Dusk Landers smiled coldly, eyes flicking from Coot to Beau to the girl and back to Coot. 'I've a

45

mind to kill you both all the same,' Dusk replied casually. 'You all right, ma'am?' he called to Sara who was staring glassy-eyed at a miracle she never expected to happen. She nodded her head dumbly, still clutching her makeshift club in case she was seeing and hearing some sort of mirage.

'So what you gonna do, Landers? Shoot a body for trying to help a poor girl in distress?' Beau said mockingly, recovered from Dusk's sudden appearance and now regarding him with cold, expressionless eyes

'Help?' Sara screamed out. 'They were going to . . . to . . .'

'I heard enough to know what they were going to do, ma'am,' Dusk replied.

'Gotta prove it first,' Beau jeered.

'Reckon Coot's got the evidence on his face,' Dusk pointed out.

'Clumsy brother o' mine walked into a thorn bush. Ain't that right, brother?'

'Sure is, sure is,' Coot cried out. 'That's the truth o' it.'

'Then we heard this scream,' Beau continued, 'an' we found this poor gal had fallen in the gully. Heard the town folks telling her not to come here on her own. It's a plumb dangerous place for a woman.' Beau smiled. 'That's the way of it an' that's all the thanks we 'uns get for saving her life.' He sounded hurt.

Sara listened speechless as the lies tripped lightly from Beau's bearded lips.

'It's not true.' She shook her head, indignation giving her added strength.

46

Dusk's eyes remained on Beau. 'Get yourself and your brother off the mountain,' he said curtly. 'An' before you leave, shuck the hardware.'

'Now wait a minute, Landers . . .' Beau began.

The Navy Colt in Dusk's hand spat flame. A mixture of dirt and sand fountained between Beau's feet, spraying over his scuffed boots, the sound of the shot echoing in the confines of the gully.

'I sure hope I ain't gotta repeat myself,' Dusk said ominously. Coot was reaching for the butt of his Colt Pioneer a second after Dusk had loosed the shot between Beau's feet. 'Real easy, Coot.' Dusk's eyes flickered on to Coot. 'Thumb an' forefinger only.'

Coot appeared only too willing to comply; the gun clattered on to the hard, stony ground at his feet and he pushed his hands high again. 'Better do as he says, Beau,' Coot called out.

'Figure that damn Injun o' yours is around some-where,' Beau said as he let the knife drop.

'Damn Injun always around. Best you not forget it,' Joe Little Wolf called from the top of the bank where Sara had fallen.

Beau smiled coldly and tossed his gun down.

'What now, Landers? What do you figure on doing wi' we 'uns?' There was no fear in Beau's voice, just a hint of mockery, for the situation had reached a stale-mate. 'Don' have you figured for being a cold-blooded killer of two unarmed men.'

Sara listened, not believing what she was hearing.

'You were going to kill me an' worse,' she stormed.

Beau's eyes fell on her. 'Don' see as you're harmed, ma'am, 'cepting by your own actions,' he

47

pointed out mildly. 'Running off like that for no reason.'

Sara's grip tightened on the limb until her knuckles were as white as the wood. 'No reason!' she stormed and Beau smiled coldly.

'Mebbe I ought to give the gun to the lady an' see if'n she agrees wi' you,' Dusk suggested. 'Move out, boys.' Dusk waved his gun to indicate a point behind him where the bank had fallen away and provided an easy climb to the top.

'What 'bout our weapons?' Beau asked. 'They cost money . . . .'

His words were cut short as the gun in Dusk's hand spat fire. The butts of both dropped Colts exploded into pieces as the guns themselves flew into the air. 'They sure do,' Dusk agreed mildly. 'Now move out, boys an' don' try anything smart, or in your case, dumb. Joe ain't as nice as me.'

They returned to the camp that Sara had set up.

'I ain't gonna be forgetting this, Landers,' Beau promised darkly.

'Well, while you're not forgetting that, here's something else to remember. Unsaddle your horses.'

The two grumbled under their breath but did as they were ordered

'I don' know what your game is, Landers, but . . .'

'That's true, you don', so now get your boots off.'

By now Beau looked fit to bust. Coot, on the other hand, never argued with a man holding a gun, nor a mean-eyed Indian and Joe was staring fixedly at him with a look that sent a shiver down his spine. He hurried to do Dusk's bidding. Beau, after a lot of arguing and threatening stood, barefooted, next to Coot, glaring hatefully at Dusk.

'OK, horseboy, you've had your fun . . . .'

'Now get on your horses an' get the hell outta here,' Dusk said, 'afore I change my mind.'

'What 'bout our saddles an' boots?' Coot wailed miserably.

'You're still alive,' Dusk pointed out. 'Think yoursel' lucky.'

'Like I said, Landers. I ain't gonna forget this,' Beau growled. He dug his bare heels into his mount's flank, starting the animal forward. Coot followed, and the two disappeared down the trail in the direction of town.

'But they should be in jail,' Sara protested. 'They were going to kill me.'

'Probably would have,' Dusk agreed as he reholstered his gun. 'But proving it would be mighty hard.'

'Why? Because I'm a woman?' she snapped back heatedly, eyes flashing.

'No, ma'am; 'cause you're still alive. Now that coffee sure smells good an' you look like you could do with some.'

She continued to glare at him and then her face softened and she smiled at him. 'You must think me very bad mannered. I'm sorry. I haven't thanked you both.'

'Coffee'll be thanks enough, ma'am,' Dusk replied, matching her smile.

Later, as night began to creep out of the trees and darken the clearing, the three sat around the fire in the gathering shadows. Coffee had turned into a meal of bacon and beans and sourdough bread. Sara had cleaned her scratches and found a fresh shirt to wear, though there was little she could do to ease the bruises and knocks that now made her body ache. To take her mind off her own discomfort, she turned to Dusk and asked:

'Why did you take their boots and saddles?'

Dusk smiled. 'The Lacey boys are ornery critters, ma'am. Be just like them to double back an' try something. Wi'out boots the hard rock hereabouts would cut their feet to pieces. They'll have to ride back to town to get more boots, an' guns if'n they've a mind too, an' I figured a long haul back down the mountain, riding bareback, will teach 'em the error o' their ways.'

'What if it doesn't?' she challenged.

'Then we'll find that out if an' when,' Dusk replied bleakly.

'I know now why the Laceys followed me, but why did you?' she asked after a few minutes' silence.

'I told you afore, ma'am, an' I reckon a lot o' folks back in town told you the same. This mountain is dangerous. It likes to kill people.'

She eyed him in amazement. 'Mountains don't have likes or dislikes, they're mountains,' she said.

'Hollow Mountain is dangerous even to men who know mountains,' Dusk went on, ignoring her objection. 'Cat, bear, timber-rattler. Then there's fires, avalanches, flash floods an' folks have been known to have been killed by lightning up here. It's not a safe place to be. Then when I heard you'd taken off for

50

the mountain alone . . .' He spread his arms in a shrug that suggested total disbelief on his part that anyone would be so stupid.

'I intend to go on and find Cajun Bokes and speak with him,' she said defiantly.

'Figured you might. But he's not that easy to find. We'll take you to him an' that at least will make sure you don' go getting lost. An' afore you go saying that you won't get lost, this is the easy part. When the trail ends, that's where God gives up an' the Devil takes over.' Dusk stared moodily into the flames of the fire as though remembering something that he'd rather forget, something that her coming up here had triggered off.

'That still doesn't answer why you followed me,' she prompted softly.

Dusk lifted his head and anger blazed in his face. 'Just trying to save you from yourself. Dammit, woman, do you wanna die?' His voice was harsh.

'I just want to find my brother,' she replied in a small voice, cowed by his sudden change of character.

'That maybe one and the same thing,' he replied roughly. He climbed abruptly to his feet. 'I'll take you to Cajun Bokes. After that you come back down the mountain wi' us an' if'n you're so set on killing yoursel', I'll hand you over to the Laceys myself. Believe me, letting them kill you is better'n having the mountain do it.' With that delivered, he stalked away from the fire and let the darkness swallow him.

She stared helplessly after him, wondering what ghosts she had awoken. Finally she settled her gaze on Joe Little Wolf, hoping that he could offer some explanation. His eyes met hers, held for an instant and then dipped and stared into the flames. Whatever was eating at Dusk would, for now, remain a mystery.

In the early hours of the morning Beau and Coot Lacey, cold and sore, arrived back at their cabin. After lighting a kerosene lamp, Beau fetched a bottle of whiskey and slumped in a chair before a battered table. Cracked and chipped china plates, food scraps dried on them, littered the table top. Beau elbowed them aside before removing the cork from the bottle, gulping at it, Adam's apple jerking up and down his scrawny throat. Finally he banged the bottle down and stared moodily at nothing in particular.

Coot had dropped gingerly into a second chair facing Beau.

'Dammit if'n I don' hurt real bad,' he moaned. 'Don' reckon I'll be able to sit a horse for a month.'

'Have drink, brother.' Ben pushed the bottle towards Coot who grabbed it up eagerly. 'You'll be riding sooner than you think.' Beau rose as he spoke and Coot followed him with questioning eyes, but Beau was saying nothing. He had moved into the shadowy rear of the cabin. As Coot pulled on the bottle he could hear Beau cussing and objects falling to the floor. Finally Beau returned. He slammed a heavy gauge, double-barrelled shotgun down on the table top. A dirty plate fell to the floor and broke. A brace of pistols, a Winchester rifle and boxes of shells followed.

Coot stared slack-jawed at this brother. 'What's going on, Beau?'

Beau dropped into his chair again, a grim, mirthless smile on his face. 'We 'uns is a-going hunting, brother.'

'Elk? Deer. . . ? Dammit, Beau, why do we wanna go a-hunting. I ain't ready to sit a saddle yet.'

'Ain't no goddam elk or deer, brother. It's one damn Injun, a sassy kid an' a she-bitch.'

Coot's jaw dropped again. 'I ain't getting what you're saying, Beau.'

Beau slammed a fist down on to the table top. Guns and plates rattled. 'We 'uns is going back up that mounain an' gonna take care o' Landers an' the other two for good,' he spat out harshly.

Alarm flared in Coot's eyes. 'Now hold on, Beau, that ain't a good idee,' he protested.

'They ain't getting away wi' what they done to us, brother. We head out at first light.'

'First light. That's almost here,' Coot squeaked unhappily.

Beau grinned evilly. 'Ain't that a fact.'

'Now hold on, brother. There's parts o' me that are near rubbed away down to the bone. I can't get on no goddamn horse. I jus' want my bed for a day or two.'

Beau laid a chilling stare on Coot who swallowed nervously under the wilting gaze. 'We 'uns got some settling-up to do that won't wait. You can have your bed, brother, until first light.' He paused and leaned forward. 'If'n you wanner stay in your bed after that, I'll put a goddamn slug in your sorry hide an' you can stay there for ever.'

Coot stared at his brother. He had never seen him so fired up before, it was frightening. Coot took a hurried pull at the bottle again, letting the fiery liquid burn all the way to his stomach.

'Ain't no need for that, Beau. I'll be wi' you,' he said placatingly.

'Figured you would, brother. Best we both get some rest now. Ain't gonna get much until we've settled our account wi' horseboy an' his Injun.'

Sara awoke the following morning to find Dusk preparing breakfast. After he had stalked out of the camp the previous evening, she had fallen asleep before he returned. She sat up and eyed him anxiously. He must have heard her moving and turned his head. His face was wreathed in a boyish grin, with no trace of whatever had affected him last night. Bacon sizzled in a pan next to a smoke-blackened coffee-pot.

'Gonna need a good breakfast, ma'am. Gonna be a day an' then afore we reach Bokes's mine an' the trail gets a little skittish later on.'

She found out what 'skittish' meant as noon approached. They had left the oaks and aspen behind as they climbed higher and now the slopes were clothed in stands of thin, graceful lodgepole pine and the thicker ponderosa pine, their scent thick in her nostrils.

The trail they were following had become little more than a narrow track as it burrowed deep into the mountains, taking them into a landscape of savage beauty and heart stopping terror. Sheer cliffs towered above them and deep gorges and ravines dropped to impossible depths. It was a beauty she could appreciate, but not when the trail became a narrow ledge, barely the width of the horse she was riding. It was at times like this that she rode with her eyes shut and hoped the horse didn't slip. There was a wider wagon-trail they could have taken, but Dusk had deliberately chosen this one, partly to teach her a lesson for the indifference she had shown to the dangers of the mountain, partly because it would have added a good four hours on to the journey.

During the ride she had no time to worry about the hurts that had left her body stiff and painful. It was only later, as once more, thankfully, pine forests closed around them, and she could relax, that her bruising and knocks made themselves felt and she was more than glad when Dusk called a halt for the day.

She slid stiffly from the saddle. 'I didn't know I could have so many places that hurt all at once,' she confessed with a groan.

Dusk laughed. 'We'll rest up here for the night, ma'am. You sit a spell while Joe an' I make camp.'

'No, I can help,' she protested, but even the task of gathering wood for the fire proved a painful chore. 'I could do with a long, hot soak in a tub,' she said.

'If'n you can stand a cold one, there's a pool in a hollow over yonder,' Dusk said, and when she showed an interest he took her through the trees to a deep, rocky hollow at the bottom of which lay an inviting pool. Dusk led her down a steep track to the edge of the pool. 'Grub'll be ready by the time you've finished,' Dusk promised and returned to the camp.

Once she was alone Sara stripped off every stitch of clothing and plunged into the pool. The coldness of the water made her gasp and stung her battered body, but after a few minutes it began to soothe the aches away. She swam for a while then floated on her back, feeling the warming rays of the evening sun caressing her body. She closed her eyes and floated until a sudden snapping of twigs on the far bank made her look up in alarm. She turned her head towards the source of the sound and screamed.

CHAPTER 5

Both men heard the scream. Dusk jumped up and cast a worried look at Joe. 'Darnit, what's she gone an' done now?' He grabbed up his rifle and with Joe following, charged towards the hollow.

The black bear, standing on all fours, surveyed her from the edge of the pool and growled softly in its throat. Only when she screamed did the animal rear up on its hindlegs, startled, waving its forepaws in the air. It shook its head and then its jaws gaped wide and it let out a bellowing roar that curdled Sara's blood. She struggled to a standing position, the water lapping at mid-thigh level.

The animal shook its head again, roared and to her horror lumbered forward, wading into the water towards her.

Dusk and Joe reached the rim of the hollow and looked down as the bear began its move towards the frightened girl. Dusk raised his rifle to his shoulder, sighting on the bear, then shook his head. The hollow was probably the bear's territory and as such the bear had first claim. He tossed the rifle into Joe's hands.

'I'll try an' scare it away. If'n that don't work then down to you,' he called as he ran to the steep path leading down into the hollow. He slid most of the way down on his backside and at the bottom let momentum keep him going.

The first Sara knew of Dusk's approach was when she heard him yelling and seconds later he splashed past her to put himself between her and the bear. The startled animal stopped uncertainly as Dusk appeared before it, the young man yelling and waving his arms. To add to the animal's confusion, Dusk pulled his handgun and fired it into the air. The yelling and the gunfire proved too much for the bear. It gave a final roar of defiance, turned and waded back to solid land. Once there it dropped back on to all fours and in great loping strides disappeared into the safety of the trees. Dusk let out a rousing 'yippee' then turned to Sara.

'Are you OK, ma'am?' His voice faded away; he had forgotten she was buck naked. His face flamed red and he hurriedly turned his back on her. 'I'm sorry, ma'am,' he apologized.

'That's all right, Mr Landers. If you could just stay there while I get dressed.'

'Yes, ma'am,' Dusk said meekly. He heard her splash her way to the edge of the pool to where her clothes lay.

'You need me anymore?' Joe called down from the rim above. Sara, not realizing he was there, gave a startled squeal, snatched up her clothes and hugged them protectively to her body.

Dusk settled his gaze on Joe. 'No!'

'I'll carry on with dinner then,' Joe replied and vanished from sight.

'You can look now, Mr Landers. I'm quite decent.' She spoke up after a few mintes.

'Obliged, ma'am.' Dusk clambered from the water. 'Best we get back to camp afore that ol' bear decides to bring his cousins along.'

'Yes. Thank you, Mr Landers, and thank you for saving me.' She gave him a quick, self-conscious but attractive smile.

'All part of the service, ma'am. After you.'

Over the meal the two men could not stop themselves from chiding Sara.

'You know, Joe. I don' know which was the most scared,' Dusk said, eyeing Sara impishly.

'Reckon the bear,' Joe replied solemnly. 'White girl, no clothes, bear run.'

Sara flushed, but a smile she was attempting to hold back to maintain her dignity, twitched her lips.

'A gentleman would have turned his back at a lady's indisposition,' she said haughtily.

Joe eyed her. 'Me no gentleman, just a goddamn nosy Injun,' he said and Dusk burst out laughing. In spite of everything, Sara found herself laughing along with Dusk and, secretly, the thought of his eyes on her naked body excited her more than she cared to admit.

Later, after the meal and while Joe tended the horses, Dusk took his coffee and disappeared from view. Sara busied herself cleaning the tin plates and cutlery. When she had finished she found herself alone, Joe had gone to the pool to get water for the horses and Dusk had not returned. After a few minutes curiosity got the better of her and she went in search of Dusk.

She found him leaning back against a tree gazing out across a deep valley at a ragged, broken peak that reared into the evening sky like an old, decaying tooth. It was an ugly-looking peak, but the rays of the setting sun, bathing it in a golden glow, softened its harshness.

'I hope I'm not disturbing you, Mr Landers,' she said softly and he turned his head in her direction; he had heard her coming.

'No, ma'am, you're welcome,' he said, giving her a smile that failed to erase a sadness in his eyes.

'I'd be pleased if you call me Sara,' she said, moving to his side.

'Only if'n you call me Dusk, ma'am . . . Sara.'

She giggled and gazed at the peak. 'Does it have a name, Dusk?'

'That's Hollow Mountain.'

'Strange name.'

'The Indians called it that because it's riddled with tunnels and caverns. To them it's a spirit place where the gods live.' There was a heavy note to his voice that she could not interpret and the sadness in his eyes turned to grief, hardening his features. His mind had drifted elsewhere, locking her out and she tried to draw him back.

'That's the second time in as many days that you've saved my life, Dusk. I'm beholden to you.'

'Glad to be of service, ma'am . . . Sara.'

'I've never met anyone called Dusk before. Is it your real name?'

He eyed her critically. 'You sure are the most questioning woman I've ever met.'

Her face fell. 'I'm sorry. I didn't mean . . .'

'Hey, it's all right,' he said cutting into her contrite apology. A smile lit up his face, chasing away the dark shadows of memory that were gathering on it. 'It was the time o' day that my ma liked the best. It was the time o' day when she could sit out and watch the sun go down. Leastaways, that's what Pa used to tell me. Ma died afore I had time to remember her, but I guess I keep her alive in my name.'

Tears sprang into her eyes. 'That's so beautiful,' she said with a choke in her voice.

'Ain't never made a girl cry afore, though,' he commented as she hurriedly wiped the tears away and smiled.

'Guess I ain't like other girls,' she replied with a laugh, but his face remained serious.

'That's for sure,' he replied softly and the way he looked at her sent a shiver down her spine and made her heart beat a little faster. She moved towards him and took the coffee-mug from his hand, placing it on the ground and her voice when she next spoke was husky.

'Like I said, Dusk, I'm beholden to you.' She stared misty-eyed into his face and before he could say anything her hands slid behind his neck, locked together and pulled his head down on to her waiting lips.

Shadows gathered in the trees and darkened as night began its rapid approach. Joe, his tasks completed, tossed a small log on the camp-fire and looked around wondering, where Dusk and the girl were. He had no worries about Dusk, but the girl could easily get lost once darkness fell. He started off in the direction he knew Dusk had taken. He had not gone far when he stopped abruptly. From beyond a dense thicket came unmistakable sounds that sent his memory back to his youth and a certain Ute maiden by the name of Dove Wing. A contented smile filled Joe's leathery, seamed face and he turned, making his way back to the camp as silently as he had come. Neither Dusk nor Sara would be needing his company at this precise moment.

'Did something happen to Dusk, up here, on the mountain?' Sara asked Joe Little Wolf the following morning. They had struck camp an hour before. Dusk had ridden ahead, as he did periodically, to check the trail, leaving her and Joe to follow at a leisurely pace.

'Why do you ask?' Joe replied guardedly.

'It's in his eyes when he looks at the mountain and it's hurting him.' She cast the Indian a sideways glance.

Joe eyed her. 'His pa died up on Hollow Mountain and he was with him when it happened. That was fifteen years ago an' this is the first time he's been back.'

She looked shocked. 'I didn't realize. It's because of me raising old memories that he's hurting inside.'

'No, ma'am. He had to return sometime, face his

demon. He's been hurting inside for a long time. Mebbe by coming up here he can drive that hurt out for ever.'

'What happened, Joe?'

Joe was silent for a moment and then he began to speak of a boy and his pa on a hunting trip, caught in a storm on the mountain and sheltering in a cave.

'He actually saw a huge, monstrous snake reach out and swallow his pa?' She could scarcely believe what she was hearing.

'Hollow Mountain is a place of powerful Indian spirits of which the snake god is one. The Indians believe the snake god lives inside the mountain.'

'But that's impossible,' she blurted out helplessly and Joe shrugged.

'Something happened that night an' Dusk's pa was never seen again. The boy saw something that terrified him an' that's the story he told. That's the memory that lives within him. The hurt that even now he has bad dreams about. He's never spoken of it since, an' mebbe this gabby ol' Indian should not have spoken of it at all.'

'I won't tell him that I know, but it helps me to know. Does that make sense, Joe?' She pulled a wry face.

Joe smiled. 'You should have been a Ute squaw,' he said enigmatically.

They entered a narrow canyon but were still able to ride side by side. As the trail descended so the walls hemming them in soared sheer to the sky. Metal horseshoes rang on stone, echoing eerily back at them from the canyon walls.

'I'd have thought Dusk would have been back by now.' Sara sounded anxious.

'Canyon long. He mebbe ride to far end. Mebbe to the Cauldron.'

'The Cauldron?' Sara turned curious eyes on him.

'You'll see it when we get there,' Joe replied. 'We will find Dusk soon. No other trail to take in the canyon. No place else to go but forward, or back.'

They found him five minutes later, but not in the manner they expected. Rounding a bend in the canyon they saw Dusk sprawled on his back on the canyon floor ahead of them. He lay still and unmoving. His horse stood a few yards from Dusk's sprawled body. The two riders reacted differently. Sara let out a startled cry and dug her heels into her mount's flanks, urging it forward, anxious to get to the prone figure.

Joe Little Wolf, more cautious, reined his mount to a halt and after scanning the upper rims of the canyon on either side, slid from his mount, pulling his Spencer rifle from its saddle sheath.

Blood matted Dusk's hair just above his left temple and he groaned as Sara gently lifted his head and rested it on her knees as she knelt by him.

'He's hurt, Joe. Help me,' she called out. Joe came cautiously forward, rifle gripped, ready to swing in any direction and she couldn't understand his – what seemed to her – reluctance.

'I allus said: the only good Injun's a goddamn dead Injun. Ain't that right, brother?'

Joe whirled about as the voice of Beau Lacey echoed sardonically from behind him. The black-

64

garbed man was grinning wolfishly as Joe turned, finger tightening on the trigger of the shotgun held hip-high. The shotgun roared and bucked. Little Wolf was lifted off his feet and flung backwards, the rifle spinning from his hands. Sara screamed.

'That's the truth o' it, Beau.' The answer came from Coot Lacey who stepped out from the rocks behind Sara, his voice mixing with the echo of the shotgun and the forlorn helplessness of the scream.

'Hey, girl, we 'uns is gonna have us a little party an' you is gonna be guest o' honour,' Beau sang out as he strode towards her.

By now Dusk was struggling to sit up, jerked back to reality by the gunshot and Sara's scream. He saw the hazy form of Beau Lacey approaching and grabbed for his gun, but the holster was empty.

'You lookin' for this, cowboy?' Beau sneered and pulled Dusk's gun from his waistband.

Dusk shook his dazed, throbbing head. With Sara's help he regained his feet.

'He shot Joe,' Sara said tearfully.

Dusk's eyes strayed to the huddled form of the old Indian lying in the dust of the canyon trail and anger surged in his eyes, driving the pain and haziness away. He took a step forward on rubbery legs.

'You won't get away wi' this, Lacey. You or your brother,' Dusk said thickly.

'Wrong, Landers, we have got away wi' this,' Beau sneered and the hand holding the pistol scythed up and across. It caught Dusk on the right cheek-bone, splitting the flesh and sending the man stumbling back until he fell to his knees. With a cry Sara threw

65

herself at Beau and he used the pistol again, slamming the barrel against the side of her head and she went down, stunned.

'Hey, Beau, this goddamn Injun's still alive. Want I should finish him off?' Coot, who had wandered across to where Joe lay, used a foot to turn the man and was surprised when the other's eyes opened. The heavy-gauge shotgun pellets had smashed the Indian's right shoulder and torn into his right cheek, shredding the flesh and turning it into a crimson, dripping shroud.

'Bring him along, brother. Like I allus say, if'n you're having a party then the more the merrier.'

CHAPTER 6

Surrounded by a circle of high cliffs, the Cauldron was a deep, sheer-sided hole that dropped a hundred feet down to where dark water, fed by a white, lacy waterfall, swirled slowly before disappearing into an unseen, underground stream. The waterfall tumbled from high up on the opposite cliff face, plunging like fine gossamer to its destination far below.

The mouth of the Cauldron was as wide as it was deep, ringed with scrub and brush. A few stands of spindly lodgepole pine grew along its perimeter and at one point an ancient oak, its trunk thick, spread leafy arms out over the Cauldron's gaping mouth. It was a place of awesome, savage beauty that at another time Sara would have enjoyed and marvelled at, but at present she was too sick with fear and worry to take in the wonder of it.

Tied hand and foot she could only watch as Beau and Coot bound and trussed Dusk, first tying his hands behind his back then binding his ankles. Finally, forcing him to a kneeling position, they used a length of rope to bind wrist and ankle bonds together. Satisfied with their work they proceeded to pass a rope across his chest and under his arms, tying it off in a loop. All the while they taunted the silent Dusk, breaking off occasionally to swig from a bottle. She could not understand the reason for the loop under his arms until Coot managed to pass one end of the rope over the end of a thick, out-thrusting limb of the oak and then both men began to haul on it.

Dusk was dragged helplessly to the rim of the Cauldron and then swung out over the hole and left to dangle some eight feet from the edge while Beau and Coot tied off the rope around the slender trunk of a lodgepole pine.

Dusk gritted his teeth as his bound legs threatened to pull his arms from their sockets as he hung in a kneeling position, the limb of the oak creaking above him.

'Ain't that just dandy,' Coot yelled out, face red and sweating from the effort.

'What are you going to do?' Sara shrilled out in dread.

'Ain't what we're gonna do, girly, it's what you're gonna do,' Beau replied.

Overhead the sun of earlier in the day had vanished behind thick, grey, menacing clouds that had drifted from the east. Though shielded from the direct rays of the sun, the heat in the Cauldron had not abated. If anything it had now increased and flies buzzed about her head which still ached from the blow she had taken.

'What do you mean?' She stared at Beau and felt a shiver of fear trickle through her as he drew his thick bladed knife. It glinted in his hand even without the touch of the sun as he stalked towards her. He grinned and then to her surprise cut the ropes that held her and hauled her to her feet, dragging her to where the tautly stretched rope suspending Dusk above the Cauldron was tied off. Her surprise and confusion increased when he dropped the knife at her feet and backed away, hooking his thumbs behind the buckle of his gunbelt.

The grin remained on his face. 'I mean that you get to cut the rope. Now ain't that good o' me?'

She shied away from the knife shaking her head. 'I'll never do that,' she said.

'Guess we 'uns'll have to change your mind,' Beau drawled. 'Bring the goddamn Injun over, brother.'

Sara half-turned to have a look as Coot dragged the blood-soaked Joe to his feet, disturbing a cloud of flies that had settled on the torn, bloody flesh of his damaged shoulder and shoved him forward. Joe Little Wolf barely had the strength to move. After two tottering steps he sank down against the bole of the pine around which the rope holding Dusk was twisted. He must have been in great pain, but he made no sound.

'Pick up the knife, girl an' cut the rope.'

She shook her head. 'I'll not do your murderous work for you.'

'That's sure a problem then. You see ol' Dusk out there is a-hurting real bad wi' his legs a-pulling on the rope. Could pull his arms clear outta their sockets an' at the same time the rope across his chest is near to suffocatin' him. The only way to relieve that pain is to cut the rope. 'Course that relief will only last 'til he hits the water then he'll have other problems to worry 'bout.'

'That's a fact, Beau, that's surely a fact.' Coot giggled, nodding.

'The other fact is that if'n you don' cut the rope, Coot here is gonna cut the Injun's eyes out. It's up to you, girl. Fact is . . . when we've cut the Injun's eyes out, I'll cut the rope mysel', so ol' Dusk, he'll be dropping no matter what.'

'You can't do that. Please,' she implored.

'Coot, you ready wi' that knife o' yours?'

'I'm ready an' rarin' to go, Beau,' Coot cried. He had hunkered down next to Joe, grabbed a handful of hair to hold his head steady and held his knife, the point less than an inch from the old Indian's right eye.

Beau stared at Sara.

'Like I said, girl. The boy's gonna die no matter what you do. Jus' depends if'n you want a blind Injun on your mind. Ain't nice to have your eyes cut out an' stay alive afterwards. Reckon it'll even make old Joe there scream. What do you say, brother?'

'He'll scream, for sure,' Coot sang out and giggled.

'Wait!' Sara cried and sank to her knees in front of the knife, staring hypnotically at it.

'Make your move, girl. Rain's a-coming in an' we wanna be away from here afore it does.' To add emphasis to his words thunder growled in the distance.

Sara picked up the knife in a trembling hand.

'Can I cut his eyes out now, Beau?' Coot called out hopefully.

'It's up to you, girl,' Beau prompted softly.

For a wild, insane second, she thought of turning the knife on Beau, but he was keeping a safe distance, making the effort a futile one. She looked at Joe, but his eyes said nothing in the grey pallor of his face. She turned her gaze on Dusk, suspended like a grotesque spider on the rope. His face was turned upwards, creased in a grimace of agony. She looked back at the rope and tears filled her eyes. She knew they were all going to die at the hands of the murderous brothers. Dusk's death would be the swiftest. She and Joe would not die so easy.

'I'm sorry, Dusk, forgive me,' she whispered and as tears blurred the rope she lifted the knife in two hands and slashed the rope. It parted with a faint twang. She dropped the knife and covered her face with her hands, sobbing uncontrollably.

Dusk was locked in a world of pain. His shoulder joints were on fire as his legs tried to pull them from their sockets while at the same time the constricting tightness of the rope about his upper chest made breathing difficult. Sweat sheened his upturned face. His ears were filled with a harsh hissing that drowned out everything but a curious popping sound coming from his left shoulder then suddenly the shoulder dissolved in a welter of pain the like of which he had never experienced before. His mouth opened and at that moment the pressure on his chest ceased and he felt himself falling, plummeting down towards the dark, swirling water at the bottom of the Cauldron.

With eyes open he watched the water rush up towards him, or that's how it seemed. He gulped air into his burning lungs, the fire in his left shoulder temporarily forgotten as he hit the water on his knees, the shock of the blow sending shafts of agony through his hips, then he was below the surface and still dropping.

He had no idea how deep the water was. He had a dreadful image of himself hitting the bottom with a force that would shatter both legs and drive splinters of bone up through his stomach. He drove the hideous thought from his mind as he sank lower and the drag of the water began to slow his descent.

The pressure of the water pushed his legs up and removed the pulling weight on his shoulders as he sank. He was conscious of the fact that as his descent slowed even further his body would try to straighten itself. The only chance he had of surviving was to somehow get his hands from behind his back to in front.

Still sinking, but getting ever slower, the water darkening around him, he thrust his behind through the loop made by his arms and pushed his arms forward. The action caused him to spin slowly, head over heels and sent waves of stabbing pain through his left shoulder.

As he reached the limit of his descent and started to slowly rise again he was now bent forward over his legs, wrists level with his ankles. The action had forced precious air from his lungs. Just a few more inches. He pushed his arms forward as far as he could, ignoring the agony that the movement caused to his left shoulder. His left arm refused to work properly so he had to work with his right. As the grey circle of the surface above grew brighter, he struggled to pull his heels through his hands. Finally he managed to draw his knees up enough to slide his heels through and his hands were before him, but still tethered by eight inches of rope to his ankles.

He broke the surface and lifted his head, enough to drag in much needed air before sinking under the surface again. Beau and Coot had missed one vital item on his person and he almost smiled under the water. There was enough rope to allow him to move his bound hands to the inside of his right boot. He dug his right hand in and closed index and middle fingers either side of the slim handle of a knife. He eased the knife up until he was able to grip it in his hand and draw it clear. It took only seconds to slip the blade behind the tether and cut it in half, freeing wrists from ankles. A few more seconds and he had sliced away the bindings at his ankles releasing his legs. Now only his wrists were bound.

He broke the surface again and this time was able to turn on his back using his legs to keep afloat. His left arm was giving him trouble. He could just about move the elbow, but the shoulder was locked and his fingers felt numb. He concentrated on manoeuvering the knife, gripping its handle in his mouth, cutting-edge upwards. Lifting his hands so that they were either side of the blade he sawed back and forth until the rope parted, releasing his hands.

Such was his concentration that only when he

passed beneath the waterfall did he realize that the current was carrying him around in a big circle. The swirling action of the water through the years had cut a deep groove around the base of the Cauldron, so he found himself floating in a channel that would hide him from anyone who might be looking down from above. Against all the odds he was still alive and a fierce wave of joy burst through his heart, but that joy was short-lived. The current was getting stronger and starting to pull him faster and he realized, with a pang of fear, he was getting near to the point where it vanished underground.

He turned over and tried to swim clear of its grip, but with only one good arm the current was too powerful. He felt panic surge through him. The current was becoming stronger, more urgent and insistent, then he caught a glimpse of the dark, narrow tunnel-mouth the water poured into. From within it came the sinister rumble and hiss of water moving rapidly.

He made one last desperate effort to swim clear but the current was too strong. He had time for one intake of air and then he was dragged, head first, into the tunnel, into a world of roaring, foaming blackness.

'Lookee at that boy go,' Coot whooped happily as the rope parted and the dangling figure dropped out of sight. 'Ain't that somethin'?' He slapped a thigh and laughed. He looked around at the bent, kneeling figure of Sara, her shoulders heaving as she sobbed quietly into her hands. Joe stared with hard, impassive eyes at Coot, causing the other to scowl. 'What you lookin' at, Injun?' He stared back at Joe, but was unable to maintain his gaze. He turned his head. 'Damn Injun's a-lookin' at me, Beau,' he complained. 'Reckon I should cut his eyes out anyway.'

Beau sniffed as overhead thunder growled. He cast an eye to the leaden clouds. 'Reckon we 'uns oughta find a dry place afore the rains come.'

'Where we gonna go, then'?'

'Ghost Canyon ain't too far. Plenty o' places there to wait out the rain.'

Coot brightened. 'Say, that's right, I 'member now.' Then his face darkened and a look of unease filled his eyes. 'Kinda spooky place as I 'member.'

Beau stared at him in disgust. 'You scared o' a few ol' Injun ghosts, brother?' he baited and Coot bridled as though he had sat on a cactus.

'I ain't scared, jus' talkin'. A body can talk, can't he?' Coot tried to hide his unease behind a belligerent reply that did not quite work.

Beau bellowed out a laugh. 'You can sure do that, brother. Now get 'em mounted an' let's get moving or we'll end up as wet as ol' Dusk. Reckon his sun's gone done for ever by now.'

Coot eyed Beau, puzzled, then a dawning light filled his eyes. 'Dusk, sundown.' He gave a bleating laugh. 'I get your meaning, Beau. Hey, that's good, real good.' He shook his head. 'You gotta quick mind, Beau. Dammit, wished I'd'a thought o' that.' He turned towards Sara, still smiling. 'You get that, girl. Dusk, sun . . .' His eyes widened and he gave a yell.

While the two had been talking her pity for Dusk and for herself turned to anger. She was dead anyway, so what did she have to lose. She picked up the knife and as Coot turned, rose to her feet, spun and lunged at him, eyes glittering.

Though he had supped enough whiskey to put most men to sleep his reflexes were diamond sharp. Beau, who was heading for his horse, stopped and turned at the sound of Coot's startled yell and saw Coot sidestep amd turn as Sara lunged. The knife snicked a button from his vest as it passed harmlessly by.

Coot grabbed her wrist in a strong, iron grip and turned it viciously, forcing her to her knees, a cry of pain escaping from her lips. The knife clattered to the ground and Coot stood over her, fury in his eyes.

'Goddam she-bitch,' he mouthed and slapped her hard across the face with two vicious slaps, one of which split her lip. He pushed her on to her back, scooped up the knife and raised a foot, ready to drive it into her ribs.

'Don' damage the goods, brother,' Beau roared out and Coot stamped his raised foot down hard on to the ground in frustration. It was a move that had him hobbling about in pain, for it was the foot she had stamped on the previous day.

'She tried to stick me,' he complained to Beau, wincing.

Beau grinned. 'She sure is a feisty woman, an' ain't they the best to have at a party?'

Coot glared down at Sara as she wiped blood from her lips with a trembling hand.

'You got some learning to do, girl, an' I'm a-gonna teach you,' he promised darkly. Grabbing a handful of hair he yanked her brutally to her feet, wringing more cries of pain from her lips.

He was no less gentle with Joe, hauling the Indian to his feet and forcing him to walk to his horse. Joe was in a bad way. The effort opened up the oozing wounds in his smashed shoulder. He coughed as he hauled himself into the saddle and gripped the pommel with his bound hands. Blood foamed on his lips, but he remained silent, holding in the pain.

Sara's hands were bound in front of her and she was forced to ride sidesaddle, holding on to the pommel as they were led away from the Cauldron. She rode beside Beau, Joe beside Coot. Dusk's mount was roped to her saddle and followed on behind.

Tears filled her eyes once more. Her own strubbornness had forced two good men to aid her. One was now dead and the other dying and soon she would be joining them, though what lay ahead for her sent a shudder of terror and revulsion through her. This time she would be on her own. There would be no white knight riding to her rescue and she was terrified.

CHAPTER 7

Dusk was carried into the thundering darkness, help-lessly caught in the flow of rushing water. In the nightmarish blackness he was tossed and turned, slammed against one wall and then another. Knees, head, elbows hit and scraped. His injured shoulder sent waves of agony rippling through his battered body. He was totally disorientated and his lungs were burning until the desire to suck in mouthfuls of water and fill his lungs with death became almost too hard to resist; then his head broke the surface.

Though he could see nothing he could feel the air on his face and gulped it in. Maybe the tunnel had widened, maybe he had entered a cave; he had no way of knowing. He reached out with his good arm: up, sideways, but could feel nothing to grab a hold of, but he sensed a slowing of the water-flow and guessed that after entering the tunnel the flow of water was branching off into smaller tunnels and easing the surge.

His knees and toes scraped the bottom. The water-level was dropping and dropping dramatically. He managed to turn his body and dig his toes in and his feet caught and held on an unseen snag. The water was now no more than six inches deep and had given up the effort of trying to drag him; instead it flowed around him. With an effort he knelt up and then sat back on his haunches. He felt himself lucky in one sense. Had there been any significant rainfall in the last few days, the Cauldron would have contained more water and probably this tunnel or cave he now sat in would have been full. On the other hand he was now deep inside the mountain with no way out and when the rains did come . . .

He sat there and put the thought out of his mind. The rumble of water was a distant, far-off sound. Within the dark confines in which he now found himself it dripped and gurgled with an eerie hollow sound. Tentatively he rose to his feet, feeling overhead for a roof, but there was nothing to impede him so he guessed that he was in a cave. He turned around slowly and a faint glimmer of light caught his straining eyes. He wondered if he was seeing things, his mind playing tricks on him, then he saw ahead, low down as he looked, the sparkle of water as the light caught it.

He moved towards the source of the light and came to a wall at the base of which yawned the mouth of a narrow tunnel which sloped steeply down. At the bottom of the tunnel the light was much stronger, but the tunnel looked awfully narrow. He eyed it thoughtfully. The source of the light was down there and indicated a possible way out, but first he had to get to it. The idea of sliding down the narrow tunnel did not appeal to him, but he had no other option.

Carefully he eased himself into a sitting position, legs in the tunnel mouth. If the tunnel was narrower than he thought and he became stuck. . . ? The consequences did not bear thinking about. His heart began to hammer in his chest and his mouth felt suddenly dry.

He inched forward, his bottom now on the start of the slope. A bit more, a bit more. . . . He couldn't stop the cry of panic escaping from his lips as he began to slide. He pulled his injured arm into his body and held it in place, hunching his shoulders as best he could.

Gravel and loose pebbles crunched beneath him. He kept his feet together and prayed. The sides of the tunnel scraped at his shoulders and began to squeeze and for one heart-stopping second he felt himself slowing. His injured shoulder cried out in agony. He wriggled his good shoulder and flailed with his heels, digging them in and bending his knees to drag himself forward. He felt that the lower half of his body was clear of the tunnel, it was his upper half that was causing the problem.

Panic built within him, a panic that he must control at all costs. He fought back the desire to scream and yell, focusing his mind, trying to ignore the wild hammer of his heart. He wriggled and pulled with his feet and legs. He was within inches of freedom, but the much narrower tunnel exit clamped down on his heaving chest. He lay there for a few seconds trying to calm himself before exhaling all the air from his chest and digging his heels in, pulling himself forward. Then he was free. He sat up abruptly, dragging air noisily into his lungs. Ahead of him an opening as tall as a man and twice as wide let in daylight from outside and he found himself in a small cave no more than ten feet wide and six feet high at its best, the roof sloping down on either side to meet the floor. The water running past him disappeared through the opening.

He picked himself up and moved towards the opening. On the edge his jaw gaped open in dismay. Beyond the cave mouth was a sheer drop of perhaps a thousand feet into a deep gorge. He was trapped with no way to escape. He retreated back into the cave. Fate was playing a nasty, cruel game with him. He dropped wearily down on to a rock and noticed for the first time that the rope used to suspend him over the cauldron was still attached to him, the chest loop having dropped down to his waist, remaining with him during his terrifying journey through the mountain. He removed it from around his waist and tossed it aside.

For the first time he was able to pay attention to his injuries. Mostly it was cuts and bruises, but it was his left shoulder that concerned him. He probed it with gentle fingers, wincing as the touch left spasms of pain in its wake. It was not hard to feel that his shoulder had become dislocated. The problem was how to get it back in place. The germ of a crazy escape plan was growing in his mind and if he was to carry it off he would need both arms in working order.

Taking a deep breath he gripped the upper part of his left arm and pulled. The effort made him cry out and sent dizzying waves of pain flooding redly through his mind. He released his grip and breathed deeply. Even that small effort had dappled his face with a beading of sweat. To get it back in position would need a sharp, powerful jerk. Outside thunder rumbled.

His eyes fell on the rope. Grimly he scooped it up and tied a section about his left wrist. He looped the other end around a rock and then sat for a few minutes composing himself. Finally, face set, he came to his feet and moved into the centre of the cave, water lapping at his ankles. He didn't think much of his impromptu doctoring, but it was the only option left to him. He bent the lower half of his arm across his heaving chest.

His thoughts turned to Joe Little Wolf, possibly dead by now, to the helpless face of Sara and finally to the two brothers, Beau and Coot Lacey, in whose hands Sara now lay. Anger swirled up through him as he thought of what they would do to her and as the anger peaked he threw himself sideways. His arm whipped out straight across his body, lifting his shoulder.

Agony ripped through his chest as his damaged arm took the full weight of his falling body. He cried out as bone grated in his shoulder followed by a popping sound as shoulder and socket reunited in a flood of screaming agony that threatened to stop his pumping heart. He spun sideways and went to his knees, his left arm extending straight out from his shoulder.

The darkness of impending unconsciousness edged into his brain. He scrabbled sideways to take the strain from his arm and scooped up a handful of water, dashing it into his face to stop himself from blacking out. It seemed to work. He came to his feet and stumbled unsteadily to where he could sit down. His whole body was trembling. He sucked air into his lungs and gently rotated his left shoulder. It worked. The dreadful pain had gone, now it was just sore. He untied his wrist and flexed the fingers. Pins and needles jabbed into his fingertips. He began to knead and rotate his shoulder and though it hurt it was a hurt he could live with. It would get better.

He sat for a few more minutes and then took himself to the cave mouth to take stock of his situation. The plan he had in mind was less appealing than his doctoring and any error on his part would mean death.

A ledge shaped rather like half a plate jutted from the base of the opening. He stepped outside and moved to one side, keeping his back to the cliff face.

The gorge spread out and away from him, running into the near distance before becoming lost in the folds of pine-clad hills. Dusk estimated that the gorge was at least a hundred feet wide. To the right, as he stood there, the wall of the gorge rose up well beyond the level of the cave. To the left, the wall was much lower, its rim broken and fanged with spears of rock and decorated with stands of pine. The cliff face he now stood on closed off one end of the gorge and the cave was centrally placed between the two walls. He studied the rock face that his back was against for a long time before returning into the cave.

The dizzying height did not worry him. He was more concerned with the ability of his left arm. For what he had in mind it would have to support his full weight at times. Allowed a few days to rest and it would be fully functional again, but that was a luxury he did not have. The rains were coming. In a few hours a raging torrent of water could be pouring from the cave mouth in what would be a most spectacular waterfall. When that happened he wanted to be long gone.

Satisfied he was as ready as he could be he returned to the entrance and turned his back on the vista of grey, gaunt peaks that were beginning to disappear into the clouds. He was about to find out how sheer the cliff face was and how good his arm was.

Thunder rumbled and echoed in his ears like deep, sardonic laughter, as though the ancient gods of Hollow Mountain found amusement at the thought of his audacious plan.

Ghost Canyon had been fashioned by the elements. Wind, snow, water, they had all had a part in forming what to Sara was as grotesque as it was beautiful.

The trail from the Cauldron had wound steadily upwards through a forest of pine, during which she had lost all sense of time. The journey seemed interminable, but it was still light when the pines ended at a towering cliff face. They entered a narrow defile that split the cliff in half and emerged a few minutes later into a weird, fairytale landscape of tall, tapering spires, graceful stone arches and huge, awning-like overhangs carved by nature at its wildest.

Here, the softer elements of the rock had been eroded and washed away to leave just the granite bones curving and arching overhead. It had taken thousands of years of tumbling, foaming water of a vast river, now long disappeared, to shape the startling landscape into what it was today: cutting into rock walls to form deep recesses, burrowing through the rock itself to shape tunnels, caves, deep vaults, all with smooth walls.

It was like riding into the skeletal remains of some huge monstrous beast. Perhaps once it had been a series of huge caverns that had, over time, collapsed in on themselves and then the water had come and washed the debris away to leave them as they stood today. Looking around at the startling structures she could relate to Coot Lacey's remark about its being 'spooky'.

Beau Lacey reined his mount to a halt and half-turned in the saddle, leering at her.

'This is where we ride out the storm, girl. Now it's party time.'

At his words Coot let out a whoop that echoed in the archways and overhangs and turned her blood cold.

Like some big spider with only four legs, Dusk inched his way across the rock face away from the cave, toes jammed into tiny crevices, fingers gripping on to even tinier ledges. From a distance the cliff face looked smooth, but close up it was lined and seamed and wrinkled like the flesh of an aged face. Sweat soaked the back of his torn shirt and trickled down his face making it itch maddeningly, but he could do nothing to relieve the terrible itching tickle other than occasionally shake his head.

It was a painstakingly slow process. The handholds were easy to find, the toeholds less so. His left shoulder ached, but so far had supported him. He estimated he had covered half the distance to the wall of the gorge, but even so it still looked a long way away. His body had taken quite a battering during the day and he was beginning to feel the effects now. He was tired and it was becoming harder to move, but still he forced himself on. If he stopped now, even for a rest, his protesting muscles would lock and eventually, inevitably, he would fall and that would be the end. A combination of determination, willpower and a burning desire for revenge on the Lacey brothers kept him going. Thunder continued to roll around the peaks, but so far the rain had kept off and he prayed that it would do so, for once the rain began it would make the cliff face slick and his tenuous grip unstable.

Doggedly he pushed through the barrier of protesting muscles and tiredness and continued his slow progress, concentrating his attention on his right hand as it led the way to safety.

As time had lost its meaning for Sara, so it had for Dusk. More than once, on the nightmare traverse of the cliff face, his feet slipped and he found himself hanging by his fingertips, but somehow he managed to recover. Then, after what seemed for ever, he looked beyond his reaching hand and elation made him almost lose his grip. The rim of the gorge was less than ten feet away. He was almost there. The realization gave him new strength and ten minutes later his feet touched firm ground and he collapsed, rolling his body away from the edge to lie flat on his back while cramps seized his muscles, making his body shake, and fatigue gripped him.

He could have lain there on the hard, wonderful ground for a year, for ever, but there were things to do that would not wait. He had to find Sara and Joe and above all, Beau and Coot Lacey. He rose on tired, rubbery legs and began his search for the others.

CHAPTER 8

The rains came as night fell. In a flash of blue-and-white, sizzling lightning followed immediately by a demonic drumroll of thunder, the heavens opened. Within the shelter of a huge cave which was open back and front the flames of a fire chased shadows back and forth around huge rock columns that rose from floor to ceiling.

Among the items Sara had brought with her were two kerosene-burning miners' lanterns and a small keg of fuel. One of the lanterns now burned on a rock ledge on the other side of the fire.

Sara sat away from the fire, back against a tumble of boulders, her hobbled feet thrust out before her, hands tied behind her back. Beau and Coot Lacey had been drinking steadily and taunting Joe Little Wolf who, against all the odds, was still alive, though barely so. Coot kicked the prone Indian in the ribs before wandering unsteadily towards the cave mouth. He came to a halt and stared out myopically through the driving rain which seemed to hang like a yellow, shimmering curtain before the cave mouth as it caught and reflected the flames.

'Lookee at the rain, Beau. Sure glad I ain't out in that.' He turned back into the cave and raised the bottle to his lips before staggering back towards the fire. He paused and stared at the girl. 'Don' you fret none, girl, we 'uns ain't forgetting you.' He belched loudly, laughed and passed on to rejoin his brother, but before he got there he tripped and fell heavily to his knees. The bottle flew from his hand and smashed on the floor, scattering dark brown shards and slivers in all directions. 'Goddammit. I hadn't finished that'un yet,' he bellowed morosely. He peered at the floor as he stood up. 'Where'd the step go I fell over?' Then he giggled and even Beau laughed.

'Seems to me you're a mite drunk, brother.'

'Could be,' Coot admitted without rancour and staggered to where Joe lay, his moccasined feet pointing to the crackling logs of the fire. He sat down cross-legged at his side, eyeing him. 'How long does it take for an Injun to die, Beau, 'cause this one sure is takin' his time?' Coot grumbled. 'It ain't no fun.'

On the other side of the Indian, Beau sat in the same cross-legged position. To Sara's eyes they resembled a pair of huge ravens eyeing a potential victim.

'Ain't no fun 'cause you bruk your bottle,' Beau pointed out and took a generous swig from his, but made no move to pass it across, making Coot more disgruntled. Coot drew out his knife.

'Think I'm gonna cut on him,' Coot announced and unfolded himself into a kneeling position.

Sara swallowed, glad she could not see what Coot was about, then her eyes caught a glimpse of something that glittered on the cave floor close to her feet and her heart leapt. It was a piece of broken bottle, curved and pointed like an arrowhead about two inches long. She heard Coot giggle at something he had done and Beau brayed out an encouraging laugh. Seeing that the two men were fully occupied she eased herself forward until she could reach the piece of broken bottle with her feet and stealthily dragged it closer.

It made a tiny tinkling sound that to her ears sounded like a peel of bells and she froze, fearful that the two had heard, but they were so intent on their own hideous business that the sound went unheard.

Lightning flashed outside and as the thunder reared and crashed she drew up her knees and back-heeled the bottle fragment closer, its tinkling journey lost in the sound of the storm.

Her heart was beating fast, mouth dry. She wriggled forward, twisted to one side and scooped up the glass fragment in her bound hands, almost crying out as the sharp point dug wickedly into her left palm, drawing blood. Keeping an eye on the two men she wriggled back to her original position.

'I wanna hear the goddamn Injun scream,' Coot said, for so far Joe had remained silent.

Beau looked thoughtful. He glanced at the fire and an evil smile tugged at his lips.

'Got me an idee, brother,' Beau declared, 'that'll make a dead man yell an' that's for sure.' Putting the

91

bottle carefully aside he staggered to his feet, moved to Joe's feet and pulled off the Indian's moccasins. Then he sat down heavily. 'Must'a fell over the same damn step you did, brother,' he commented and both men broke into peels of drunken laughter. When they had finally recovered Beau continued. 'Reckon this ol' man's feet are cold. Could do wi' a little warming up.' He nodded his head at the fire and a slow smile of understanding spread across Coot's whiskey-inflamed face. He stared at Joe.

'We're gonna warm your feet up, Injun. Now ain't that right neighbourly o' us.'

Sickened at what she was hearing and what they intended to do, Sara intensified her efforts to cut the bonds at her wrists. She had managed to wedge the bottle fragment in a crack at the base of the rock and while the two had been talking and laughing she had been sawing the rope back and forth against the edge of the glass. More than once the sudden pain as she caught her wrists on the jagged edge almost made her cry out, but she managed to stifle the impulse. Now she redoubled her efforts, throwing caution to the wind in her attempt to escape.

'Reckon he ain't too pleased at the idee, Beau,' Coot sang out and before Beau could frame a suitable reply a low, sing-song chant broke from Joe's dry, bloodied lips.

Coot staggered to his feet. 'Why's he singing, Beau?' he demanded nervously.

' 'Cause it's a party,' Beau suggested lightly.

'Well, I ain't liking it.' To match his words he drove a foot into the Indian's side. 'Quit the noise, ol'

92

man.' But Joe continued, unintelligible words rising and falling.

'I said to quit it,' Coot screamed out and twice more his foot crashed into the side of Joe's ribcage, the second time accompanied by the ominous crack of breaking bones. This time Joe did stop and rolled his head to stare up at Coot.

'This is my place, this is my land,' he croaked. 'The spirits are here to guide me on my way. You will die here, both of you. The spirits speak. The mountain wants your blood.' Joe turned his dying gaze upwards as he finished. His words, though softly spoken, were heard crystal-clear by both men.

Coot backed away and stared crazily at his brother. 'Did you hear that, Beau? He said we're gonna die.' Panic edged his voice and flashed in his eyes. 'He's done put a curse on we 'uns.'

Beau weaved to his feet. 'Then I guess we'd better uncurse oursel's, brother. Grab a leg.'

The two dragged Joe towards the fire and then let his feet drop into the flames, scattering the logs as they settled into the glowing embers beneath.

If Joe felt the pain as the flesh on his feet began to blister and pop, he gave no sign. There was a half-smile on his face that remained as, a few minutes later, his head lolled to one side and his eyes glazed over. Death had finally claimed Joe Little Wolf.

'Dammit, he's dead,' Beau said callously. 'Hey, girl, it's your turn to join the party now,' he called. His jaw dropped. Sara had gone.

Dusk made his way back to the Cauldron, not

surprised to find it deserted. He was now faced with a problem. Which way had they gone? Back down the mountain or up? He found the answer a few minutes later. After casting around he came upon fresh hoof-marks and droppings on the trail which he knew led to Ghost Canyon. Though he had only been a boy the last time he had been up here, he remembered it all. With the threat of impending rain, the canyon offered the only possible shelter and it was where he would have made for. Dusk knew that it was a long, uphill climb to the canyon, but resolutely set off in that direction, knowing that he would not get there before nightfall. He had covered about half the distance when the storm that had been threatening all the afternoon broke and reminded him of a night, a long time ago, that he would have preferred to forget.

Sara had made good her escape from the cave at about the time Joe began his chant, edging back into the shadows after cutting through her bonds, making her way to the open rear of the cave and the storm-riven darkness beyond. Her encounter with the storm was a brief skirmish as she passed through a ragged curtain of water beneath two opposite over-hangs that did not quite meet in the middle, and entered the dark maw of another cave. Here she paused uncertainly as her vision of escape evapo-rated in the impenetrable darkness that surrounded her.

Unable to see what lay ahead she felt a flood of hopelessness wash over her; then, from outside a flash of lightning lit up her surroundings for one garish second, penetrating holes and cracks in the roof above. In that brief instant she saw ahead of her a forest of thin-waisted columns rising from floor to ceiling where stalactites and stalagmites had met and joined together. Where they did not meet the roof was covered with spear-tipped stalactites of varying length reaching down to bulbous-based stalagmites. It was like being in the mouth of a monstrous, sharp-toothed predator.

The cave was big, its walls oozing with overlapping cushions of smooth, white rock which were shrouded in a cape of glistening water. Water dripped and gurgled from every direction, but before the lightning flash died, she had fixed her course, heading towards the rear of the cave where briefly she had glimpsed a number of dark openings.

'Damn the girl. She's always a-running off,' Beau raved.

'It ain't fair,' Coot moaned.

'Git that other lamp lit, brother, an' we'll go find her. She ain't gonna get far.' Beau laughed. 'Ain't nowhere for her to go. An' when we find her. . . ?' He didn't need to elaborate and Coot grinned as he scampered off to get the other lantern.

Some time was lost as he attempted to fill the lantern from the keg, spilling a lot of the fuel and cursing, but at last the second lamp was lit and with each carrying one the two set off in Sara's wake. It was not difficult to find out which way she had gone. In the second cave, though water dripped and ran, raised areas of the floor were relatively dry and they were able to find her wet footprints. Beau grinned wolfishly.

'Here we 'uns come, girly, ready or not,' he sang out loudly, his voice echoing in the darkness beyond the glow of the lamps. Coot giggled.

Dusk reached Ghost Canyon, dripping and sodden, a state he had grown used to. He found the cave easily, drawn there by the still flickering fire. He stood now, looking down at the still, dead form of Joe Little Wolf, tears of grief and anger mingling with the rain-water that ran down his cheeks.

Apart from the old man's feet, which had been reduced to ash-covered bone emerging from blistered, charred fresh, his chest had been sliced open in more than a dozen places. Dusk stood in shock for a few minutes before dragging the body clear of the fire and folding the arms across the ruined flesh. Joe's face was serene, calm and still decorated with the tiny smile. Dusk closed the open eyes and then went across to where the saddles had been dumped, found a blanket and draped it over the body.

He moved around the cave. Everything told a story. The smashed whiskey bottle, spilt oil. He found the fragment of glass stained with blood. Sara had got away. Hurry or drunkenness had caused someone to spill the kerosene while filling the lamps, probably both. Now the brothers had gone in search of the missing girl.

All the tiredness had gone from his body and a new-found energy gave an urgency to his moves. He went to his own saddle-bags and pulled out a pair of calf-length, hide moccasins that Joe had made for him. He tore off his boots and drew the moccasins on. They would allow him to move silently. He found his gunbelt and strapped it on along with Joe's big, broad-bladed hunting-knife and as an afterthought, he grabbed up a coiled picketing-rope. Stripping off his torn, soaking shirt he tossed it aside and returned to the fire. Here, face hard and emotionless, he knelt down and rubbed his fingers in the cool, grey ash around the edges of the fire.

He drew lines on his face, one on each cheek and one across his forehead and a final one down the middle of his chest. He could not explain his action except to say that it felt right. In a single instant he had changed from a civilized man into a savage with only one dark thought driving him on. He looked across at the shrouded form.

'Goodbye, old man, friend, father.' His voice cracked a little. 'My heart is with you for ever.'

Lightning flashed and thunder growled outside. The horses, bunched together, whickered nervously. They looked across the cave towards the dying fire where the man had been. He was gone and they were alone once more.

CHAPTER 9

The lightning aided Sara in her flight. Every now and again a flash would penetrate into her dark world through a hole or fissure and give her the briefest glimpse of her surroundings. Enough to allow her to progress deeper into the warren of tunnels and caves in this impossible place.

So far she had been able to keep going as there had always been a way out. It was like passing through an old, deserted house, going from room to room, along corridors. Sometimes going up, sometimes going down. Now she had entered the last room and from this there seemed to be no way out other than by the way she had entered.

It was a high, lofty cave filled with weird, white, water-sculpted rock formations and clusters of hanging, dripping stalactites. The centre of the cave had fallen away into a deep pit ringed with a wide ledge and up from the pit echoed the gurgle and splash of running water. Had it not been for the lightning entering through a crack in the roof she would have fallen into the pit. Now she waited for the next lightning flash, hoping that an as yet unseen exit would present itself, but when the flash came there was nothing. She had come to a blind end. Her only hope was to hide and pray they would not find her.

In places the salts washed out of the rock had rolled across the ledge and down the side of the pit like wax from a melting candle. As footsteps echoed and the glow of a lantern flared from the tunnel by which she had entered, she scrambled quickly across one such formation and hunkered down in a niche behind some rock columns and waited with bated breath, hoping the drumming of her heart was not as loud as it sounded to her.

'Damn girl. She could be anywhere,' Coot moaned, twenty minutes into the search.

'Patience, brother,' Beau soothed. 'We 'uns will find her.'

'Supposin' we don'? She could'a fell down a hole an' bruk her fool neck. Be somewhere outside in the canyon. Mebbe she was hidin' an' we passed her by an' now she's on her way back to the cave for her horse so she can skedaddle outta here.'

'You worry too much, brother,' Beau replied. He came to a halt and swung around on Coot. 'We'll split up. Cover ground quicker that way. Just holler if'n you find her. An' don' worry. You can't get lost in here.'

'So you say,' Coot replied worriedly.

'Ain't scared, are you, brother?' Beau asked slyly.

'No, I ain't scared,' Coot snapped back.

'Like I said, holler if'n you find her an' I'll do the same.'

Left alone, the walls pressed in around Coot as he made his way nervously along a tunnel, the lantern surrounding him in a cocoon of dirty, yellow light. Sounds pitched in his ears and fired his nerves to jumping point. Fully sober now, sweat beaded his upper face beneath the brim of his hat.

Lightning flashed ahead and thunder rolled along the tunnel. Dammit! The girl wasn't worth all this aggravation. She was either dead or not in these caves, and not in these caves was where he wanted to be right now. He rubbed sweat from his eyes. He had an uncomfortable feeling that he was being watched.

He emerged from the tunnel onto a broad ledge which ended at the lip of a huge, yawning shaft that went so far down that he could not see the bottom. He was in an immense cavern which, besides being bottomless, had no walls or roof that the meagre glow of his lantern could pick out. He swallowed and backed away from the edge. He had had enough. Beau could do what he wanted, he was out of here. He turned to retrace his steps and his eyes widened in terror.

A figure stood in the tunnel mouth, a hideous, painted figure that he recognized and knew he could not be seeing.

'Hello, Coot. Fancy meeting you here,' Dusk said in a soft, mocking tone.

Coot Lacey could only stare with popping eyes at the terrible apparition, the sound of his madly drumming heart beating in his ears. His body shook and his legs refused to support him. He went to his knees, still holding the lantern out before him.

'You're dead,' he whispered hoarsely.

'No, Coot, you are,' Dusk replied coldly, stepping before the terrified, kneeling man and coolly taking the lantern from him, setting it down on the floor.

'You're dead!' Coot repeated, his voice an octave higher and close to madness.

'The old man had done nothing to you,' Dusk said stonily. He removed Coot's hat, tossing it into the shaft before placing a loop of the picketing rope around his neck. 'The girl had not harmed you.' Dusk turned the other end of the rope around an upthrusting spur of rock and tied it off, his eyes only leaving the unresisting man for the briefest of seconds. Now he hauled him to his feet. 'Was he still alive when you put his feet into the fire?'

'It was Beau, it was Beau,' Coot shrieked. Spittle flew from his lips in a burst of foul breath as his accusation echoed and re-echoed in the black vastness of the cavern. He broke free from Dusk's grip and stepped back. 'Am I . . . am I, dead?' Coot asked dazedly. He seemed oblivious of the rope about his neck.

Dusk took a step towards him; Coot stepped back once more but there was nothing under his foot. With a cry he fell into the blackness of the chasm. The coil of rope at Disk's feet followed him, then went taut with a faint twang.

Below the ledge, in the shrouding, swallowing darkness the body of Coot Lacey swung jerkily back and forth, legs kicking. The fall had not broken his neck, but left him to the more prolonged agonies of slow strangulation. He clawed at the rope, his restricted breathing harsh. Dusk stood on the edge of the ledge for a few moments listening to the tortured breathing, no sign of remorse on his hard, set face before returning to where the rope was tethered. He pulled out Joe's hunting knife and sliced the rope in two.

'You are now,' he said in a soft, belated response to Coot's last question and turned away, picking up the lantern. Supernatural dread had turned Coot into a terrified puppet who had offered no resistance. Dusk doubted that it would be the same with Beau.

Sara peeked from her hiding-place. Beau stood within the cavern, lantern raised, its lambent, yellow glow bathing him in a soft, sulphurous light. He peered around intently, but the glow of the lantern did not reach as far as her corner. Even so, she shrank back when he appeared to be staring directly at her.

'Ain't nowhere to go, girl. I know you're in here.' His voice echoed with a hollow tone. 'Best you step out now an' save yoursel' a whole heap o' grief.'

Sara trembled in her niche. How could he know she was in here? He had to be bluffing, trying to force her to show her hand. She remained still hands pressed to her mouth.

'You can't hide for ever. Me an' brother Coot, we'll find you soon 'nough, make no mistake.' He gave a sinister chuckle.

Lightning flashed and filled the cavern with its

garish light, springing dark shapes from the stalactites to paint black shadows on the white walls. It lit her up starkly in her corner and a gasp flew unchecked between her covering fingers before it was drowned by a shattering peel of thunder that reverberated around the cavern before fading away. Small though the sound she had made had been, Beau's straining ears had caught it and a wolfish smile filled his face as the thunder rolled about him.

'That's plumb neighbourly o' you to let me know where you're at, girl,' Beau called as the thunder faded away. He began to move around the edge of the pit in her direction, but her eyes were straining beyond him at something she had seen in the lightning flash. A trick of the light, it had to have been, but it had caused the gasp and betrayed her position.

'Wait until I tell brother Coot,' he sang out, 'he'll be as happy as a hound-dog wi' a bone an' that's the truth o' it.'

'Brother Coot's not interested in anything any more,' a voice cut in and Beau turned. Sara's heart jumped for joy. It had not been a trick of the light, for there, standing at the limit of the glow thrown by the lantern, stood Dusk. In his hand he held his Navy Colt and now he thumbed back its hammer in a series of dry clicks. The lantern he had taken from Coot he had left further down the tunnel before following the sound of Beau's taunting voice.

'Dusk!' Sara cried out the name in joy and relief and came to her feet.

'Stay where you are, Sara,' Dusk called out, not taking his eyes from Beau. She remained where she was, looking down on the two men.

Beau let surprise widen his eyes for a few seconds as he took in the half-naked figure daubed with grey lines.

'Hell, boy, how'd you make it back from the Cauldron?'

'I'd tell you if'n you had that much time left,' Dusk replied bleakly.

'What have you done wi' Coot?' Beau asked.

'He was hanging around for a while, then we parted company. He went to hell an' I came looking for you.'

Beau nodded. 'Coot must' a figured you wus a ghost. Reckon you done scared him to death, what wi' them Injun markings an' all.' He gave a chuckle and stared brightly at Dusk. The fear so evident in the late Coot Lacey did not exist in Beau. 'So what do we do now, Landers? You gonna jaw me to death or are you gonna arrest me?' There was a mocking note in Beau's voice.

'No, I'm gonna kill you,' Dusk replied.

'You could do,' Beau agreed, 'but you won't. I figure you for one o' them fair men. It ain't in your nature to gun a body down wi'out a chance.' Raising his gun hand well clear of his holstered weapon he bent, placed the lantern on the floor between them and straightened, holding both hands at shoulder level. He stepped back a pace or two from the lamp and gave a snorting laugh. 'See what I mean. If'n I had had the drop on you, I'd'a put a bullet in you when you bent.'

'Joe never had a chance. He died hard an' in

agony,' Dusk said coldly.

Beau shrugged. 'That's me, I guess, the way I am an' the way you are is that you gotta give me a fair chance. Lower the gun an' let me make a play for mine. The winner gets the girl. Now that's fair.' He gave a grin that turned to pain and shock as the Navy Colt bucked and spewed flame in Dusk's hand and a bullet smashed into Beau's right hip, shattering the bone.

Beau staggered and went to his knees, clutching at the wound with both hands, staring at Dusk in disbelief.

'You got me figured wrong, Beau. I stopped being a fair man when you an' your brother killed Joe.' Dusk fired again. The bullet missed Beau, but then he was not firing at the kneeling man.

The glass barrel of the lantern shattered. The lantern spun on to its side but the flame did not go out. It flickered wildly, sending drunken, dancing shadows over the nearby wall. Dusk fired again as Beau freed a bloodstained right hand to claw at his own gun.

The lantern leapt into the air as the bullet punctured the oil reservoir. Kerosene splashed over Beau's bent knees and ignited with a dull whoosh. Beau had managed to draw his gun but dropped it as flames danced up from his lap. He staggered to his feet, clutching his right hip with his left hand while trying to beat out the flames with his right.

'Help me!' he shrieked.

A pool of kerosene at his feet burst into flame, engulfing Beau's lower half. He screamed and tried to stagger clear of the flames. He managed a few steps before his right leg collapsed under him and he fell sideways, sprawling on the edge of the pit. With a despairing cry he toppled in.

Dusk moved to the edge of the pit. Beau lay some twenty feet below him, his own burning body providing enough light for Dusk to see that the other's luck had really deserted him. Beau had skewered himself on a slender stalagmite. It had pierced his lower back and now jutted some eight inches from his stomach. He twitched feebly, the lower half of his body wrapped in flame. The smell was awful, rising from the pit as flesh crisped and fat boiled, flames flaring as blisters exploded with a dull pop.

'Help me!' Beau's weak, pain-racked words reached Dusk's ears, but Dusk felt no pity for the man.

'I'm helping you like you helped Joe. Say hello to Coot for me.' Dusk turned away from the edge. Thunder beat out a reverberating drum roll, drowning out the hiss and pop of burning flesh and the weak, gurgling cries of the dying man.

Sara scrambled from her hiding place and threw herself into Dusk's arms.

'I thought you were dead,' she sobbed, hugging him tight as though to convince herself that she was not dreaming.

'So did I,' he replied.

As Beau died so the adrenalin-charged strength ebbed out of Dusk, leaving him tired and drained to the point of exhaustion. They returned to the outer cave. Sara spent a few minutes adding a few sticks of dry wood which had been gathered earlier to the glowing embers of the fire. Dusk flopped to the floor. When she turned back to him she found that he had fallen into an exhausted sleep.

The rain fell ceaselessly all night though the boisterous heart of the storm had drifted away. It stopped just after sun-up and a watery sun peered hazily through the veil of cloud.

Dusk awoke with the sun and while Sara slept on he found the time to bathe his stiff body in a pool of icy water and put on a fresh set of clothes taken from his saddle-bags. Apart from a stiffness in his left shoulder from the dislocation, the rest of his injuries were mainly ugly patches of yellow and blue bruising along with a few cuts and grazes that would soon heal.

Sara struggled from a deep sleep with the smell of coffee filling the air. Dusk glanced around as she sat up, a boyish smile on his face. Gone was the demonic, vengeful killing-machine of the night before and returned was the kind, charming young man.

Sara insisted on making breakfast and afterwards Dusk attended to Joe. He placed the old Indian's body on a high ledge at the back of the cave and with Sara's help covered it in a cairn of rocks. There were no prayers said, just a few simple words of goodbye that left Sara misty-eyed and feeling choked. As they prepared to leave Sara approached Dusk and laid a hand on his arm.

'I'm so sorry about Joe, Dusk. It's all my fault that he's dead.' Her voice faltered and broke and tears sprang into her eyes.

Dusk smiled and cradled her chin with a hand, forcing her head up to look into her watery eyes.

'Indians believe in fate. Joe would have said that this was meant to be and he died where he wanted to be. This is his place.'

Tears rolled down her cheeks.

'He told the brothers that just before he died. He also told them that they would not leave the mountain alive. How could he know?' She searched his face for an answer.

Dusk drew his hand away and shrugged.

'Only an Indian can answer that for you. Let's get out of here.'

'I'll be glad to get back to town, away from this place,' she said, rubbing her eyes.

'Town?' He cast her a glance. 'That can wait a spell. You came up here looking for your brother, so we'll do just that. Reckon Joe would have wanted it that way. We'll head over to Cajun Bokes' mine. It's only two, mebbe three hours' easy ride from here.'

'Are you sure?' she questioned.

'Reckon to see this thing out,' he replied with a nod as he swung astride his mount. 'Figure there's nothin' else that can happen to us.'

It was a statement that he would soon regret making.

They rode out of Ghost Canyon leading the packhorse and the mounts of Joe Little Wolf and the Lacey brothers. Dusk had discarded the saddles and used a simple halter rope to lead the animals. It was not that he wished to be burdened by the extra animals, but up here was not horse country and if he left them to their own devices they would soon die.

Thunder growled softly in the far distant peaks to the north as above them the sun broke through the torn, ragged clouds in golden shafts. Dusk glanced up at the sky as they emerged from the canyon on to the sweet-smelling, pine-clad slopes. The clouds were grudging on the amount of space they allowed the sun and he reckoned there would be more rain by nightfall.

CHAPTER 10

'Git your hands up! I'm ready to shoot anyone who's on my land wi'out my permission.' The waspish, snarling voice could have come from any direction, but Dusk made no immediate effort to locate the whereabouts of the hidden owner of the voice. He made no effort to comply with the command, either, as he reined his mount to a halt.

'Ease up on the trigger, Bokes. It's Dusk Landers. I'm here to talk a spell an' ridden a long way to do it.'

'Then you can turn 'round an' ride back. If'n I wanna talk I'll go to town, if'n I don' then I'll stay here. I don'.'

Dusk sighed and cast a bemused Sara a quick, amused glance. They had arrived at a wide clearing. Three sides were thickly forested with pine. Ahead of them, the fourth side was a cliff of grey rock breached by a square, dark opening. To one side lay a small log cabin ringed with unkempt, tangled weeds that curled up over the veranda and entwined their way up the overhang supports. Opposite the cabin lay a flatbed wagon, blue paint peeling from its low sides, slowly sinking into a sea of weeds.

Mounds of rock, brought from within the mine, littered the ground to the right of the mine entrance. On some the resilient plant life had established a hold, others were newer, fresher.

Dusk swung himself out of the saddle and stood, easing the kinks from his back.

'Ain't said you could git down,' the hidden voice said truculently.

'Show yoursel', Bokes. I don' like talking to thin air,' Dusk called out.

'Landers. You're that horse rancher fella. Well, if'n you're selling, I ain't buying an' if'n you're buying, I don' got none to sell. Is that talking enough?'

'Reckon I just 'bout got it figured where you are, Bokes. Figure if'n I draw an' fire three shots at least one will hit that mean old hide o' yours. The lady here would like to ask you a few questions.'

'Lady? What lady?'

'This lady,' Sara yelled out and pulled the hat from her head, shaking her hair free.

Cajun Bokes rose into view. He had been crouching behind a stand of low brush near to the wagon. He toted an old shotgun, but its barrel was now pointing to the ground.

'Didn't recognize you for a lady, ma'am,' he growled, squinting up at her with dark eyes set in a weather-beaten face, 'being as you're dressed like a man.' He scowled at her. 'Heard you allus rode wi' an Injun?' He eyed Dusk.

112

'He died,' Dusk said abruptly. 'Now I ride alone.'

'So what do you wanna jaw 'bout?'

'Coffee would be nice around 'bout now,' Dusk pointed out.

'You said jaw, nothin' 'bout coffee,' Cajun Bokes returned acidly.

'Well, now I'm saying coffee. We been in the saddle close to four hours. Figure to take it easy for a spell.'

'You figure a lot. Next you'll be wantin' to stay the night.'

'Kind o' you to offer,' Dusk said with a smile.

'I didn't,' Cajun barked back. 'This ain't no fancy hotel. State your business an' then ride out. I got work to do.'

Dusk looked across at Sara who had, by now, dismounted.

'Cajun here is noted for the warmth of his greeting an' hospitality o' his table.' His words brought a giggle to Sara's lips and a frown to Cajun's face. He stared suspiciously at Dusk.

'What you got all them horses for?'

'Had a run-in wi' a couple o' bad men who took it real personal when we wouldn't die,' Dusk said bleakly. 'Had to teach 'em the error o' their ways.'

Cajun sniffed. 'Guess they learned the hard way.'

'You could say that,' Dusk agreed.

'Anyone I might have knowed?'

'Beau an' Coot Lacey.'

'They're real mean boys,' Cajun said with a nod.

'Were,' Dusk corrected.

'So, what do you want to know from me?'

113

'Let's have that coffee. Need to rest the horses a spell. Get 'em fed an' watered.'

'This ain't no livery stable, neither,' Cajun began, annoyance clouding his voice.

'Ease up, Cajun. Got somethin' for the use o' your time.' Dusk moved across to the pack-horse and returned with a bottle of whiskey. It had once belonged to the Laceys. He handed it to Cajun who took it appreciatively.

'Let's get that coffee then,' Cajun offered grudgingly.

'. . . That's why I wanted to talk with you, Mr Bokes. The people in town said that my brother and his friends talked to you before they set out looking for Brogan's gold,' Sara explained later within the confines of the cabin, seated at a rough table. Cajun Bokes sat opposite her while Dusk was content, leaning against the back wall, sipping his coffee and listening. 'Mebbe I did, mebbe I didn't. Talk to a lotta folk when I go to town. When would this have been?'

'Three, four months ago.'

Cajun sniffed and shrugged. 'Like I said, ma'am. Talk to a lotta folks when I go to town.'

'Three young men. Tobe Kellman, Frank Tooley and Mort Simmons,' she prompted anxiously.

'Can't say I did, can't say I didn't. Lotta folk come a-looking for Brogan's gold. I allus tell 'em to ride on back from where they came, but they never do.' He shook his head resignedly.

'Anybody come visiting you here, at the mine?' Dusk spoke up.

114

'You're the first folk I've seen since I was last in town. Nobody comes up here, an' that's the way I like it. If'n you folks wanna find a dry campsite afore dark, you best leave now. Rain'll be coming in agin, tonight.' Cajun rose to his feet and shrugged himself into a coat that was hanging on a peg behind the door. 'Got me some work to do.'

Dusk drained the last dregs of coffee. 'Thanks for your time an' the coffee.'

' 'Bliged to you for the whiskey. Keep to the trail an' follow it south at the big oak. Take the east fork an' you'll end up in Echo Canyon an' that don' lead nowhere. It's a box canyon. One way in an' the same way out. Don' say I ain't warned you.'

'I'll remember,' Dusk promised as he led Sara from the cabin. Sara turned as the two stepped into a brief period of sunshine.

'Are you sure Tobe and his friends did not come here, Mr Bokes?'

'I said not.'

'Or you didn't meet them on the trail?' Her voice sharpened and Dusk gave her a quizzical, puzzled, glance. Cajun Bokes' glance was hostile.

'I've already said my piece, ma'am an' it ain't gonna change.'

'I'll get the horses,' Dusk said waving away from the two, wondering about her change of tone as he headed to where the horses waited. His journey took him close to the mine entrance and as he passed it he came to a sudden stop and stared in. There was nothing for him to see, but it was his hearing that was trying to tell him something.

He strained his ears, listening, but the sound that had stopped him was not repeated; maybe he had imagined it.

'Horses ain't in the mine,' Cajun shouted. Dusk waved a hand and continued on to where the horses grazed and led them back to where Sara and Cajun waited.

'You got a partner here, Cajun?' Dusk asked.

Cajun glanced warily at him. 'Ain't got no use for partners. Why do you ask?'

'Thought I heard the sound of a pick hitting rock when I passed by the mine entrance.'

'Old mines make funny noises,' Cajun said quickly, ' 'specially after heavy rain. Like as not water dripping.'

'Guess you're right,' Dusk agreed as he swung into the saddle.

'Know I am,' Cajun growled. ' 'Member what I said. Fork right at the oak. Echo canyon can be a real dangerous place if'n you get caught in there when the rains come.'

'I hear you, Cajun. 'Bliged for your time.'

Cajun Bokes stood and watched them leave, remaining there long after they had vanished from sight until he was satisfied they would not return. Then he picked up his shotgun and headed to the mine.

'He's lying, Dusk,' Sara said with conviction, once out of sight of the mine. Dusk cast her an enquiring glance. That coat he was wearing. It was Tobe's, I'm sure of it.'

'There's something going on up there,' Dusk said with a nod. 'I heard a pick being used in the mine, no matter what Cajun said, so why's he being so darned secretive 'bout it?'

'What are we going to do?'

'Firstly, take a look at Echo Canyon. He was mighty insistent that we keep away from the canyon. 'Pears to me we should take a look.'

The clouds were building and merging into a leaden canopy overhead when the two rode down the steep, narrow incline between high walls that led into the canyon. At the bottom of the incline the walls shrank back on either side to reveal the canyon itself. A deep fissure in the earth surrounded by high, sawtooth ridges. It was perhaps some 200 yards wide and half a mile long, choked with brush and scrub. Dusk had tethered the other horses in a small clearing at the head of the canyon. Water rushed somewhere to their left, hidden by the dense undergrowth. Insects buzzed in the humid silence and birds screeched out of the trees as they passed. The sound of metal-shod hoofs rang back at them from the high, grey walls. Thunder growled menacingly from beyond the western rim.

The trail they followed was narrow, no more than an animal run, forcing them to ride in single file as it meandered towards the closed end of the canyon.

'What are we looking for?' Sara called after a while and the canyon repeated her words.

'Ain't too sure, but I figure we'll know it when we find it,' Dusk said unhelpfully.

They found it twenty minutes later in a rocky

117

hollow to the right of the trail. Through a thin, ragged screen of brush a white mesh caught Dusk's eye. He slid from his mount, telling Sara to remain in the saddle while he had a look. He pushed the brush aside and the sight that caught his eyes stunned him. The hollow was filled with the bones of dead horses. The white 'mesh' he had glimpsed was the fleshless ribcage of a horse. In the macabre, animal graveyard he estimated that there were the remains of at least twenty horses.

They lay tangled together, horseshoes rusting on bony feet. Some had been there for years, others newer, partially clad in dry, brittle flesh. He had never seen anything like it before and the horror was compounded by the fact that rotting saddles were still cinched about fleshless ribcages. Sara cried out in disbelief and covered her mouth with a hand, eyes popping at the tragic, terrible sight that was revealed as Dusk broke through the brush.

Dusk slithered down into the hollow and was greeted by the final horror. Each animal skull, or as many as he could see, had been shattered by a bullet. The horses had been deliberately slaughtered. The terrible sight brought a mistiness to his eyes that he rubbed away as anger surged through his breast at the callous butchery. He clambered back on to the trail, face grim and hard.

'Guess a man who can kill helpless animals needs some serious investigating.'

'What's that over there, Dusk?' Sara pointed ahead and to the right at something that he could not see and wished he had not a few minutes later as he

118

stood on the edge of a shallow pit. Finding the dead horses had been bad enough. In the pit were the bones of a dozen men clad in tattered clothing. Fleshless, grinning faces staring up. Dusk tried to keep her away, but was too late. She clung to him, staring white-faced into the awful pit.

Like the horses some of the bodies were newer additions to the mass grave. One in particular made her cry out and she would have fallen had not Dusk grabbed her. Leathery flesh had pulled tight around the skull of this one and clumps of dark hair wove a dark web about the shrunken features. He lay sprawled on his back atop the pile of bones where he had been casually thrown.

'That's Frank Tooley, one of Tobe's friends,' her voice, barely above a whisper, shook. She buried her face in his chest.

'Are you sure?' he asked and she nodded.

There was another body there and, judging by the state of the clothing, it could have been put there about the same time as Frank Tooley, but the skull was crushed. It lay face down with Frank Tooley's legs across its back. Dusk made her look again to see if she could recognize the clothes of the second man, but she could only shake her head dumbly. She couldn't tell if it was her brother or not.

Dusk drew her away from the dreadful charnel pit. The sight of first the slaughtered horses and now the murdered men – he could only conclude they had been murdered – had shaken him up and he was trembling himself. What in dear God was going on here? Why? Why? Why?

119

'Let's get outta here,' he said thickly. 'We'll pay Cajun Bokes a second visit, but this time we'll wait until dark. I want to have a look in that mine o' his.'

Night had fallen and with it came the rain beating noisily on their yellow slickers as they slipped into the mine. Dusk had tethered the horses in a clearing down the trail and with Sara had completed the final approach to the mine on foot. Cajun Bokes was in his cabin. Dusk had risked a quick peep through the window; the old miner was seated at his table eating by the light of a kerosene lamp. Any sound they might have made was covered by the drumming of the rain and the rumbling growl of thunder. Once safely inside the mine the two slipped out of their slickers and Dusk hid them behind a rock. He had brought along a lantern, but did not risk lighting it until they were well away from. the entrance.

Water dripped and trickled around them and glistened on the rough grey walls. In the yellow glow of the lantern the darkness ahead retreated only to pile in behind theme. Shadows flared and danced nervously about them. The curving tunnel they followed ended at a hole in the floor with the top of a crude, wooden ladder projecting from it. Soundlessly Dusk descended the ladder, which dropped down ten feet or so into a wide, natural tunnel below. To the left, as he faced the ladder waiting for Sara to join him, the tunnel narrowed and after a few yards ended. To the right, as far as he could tell, the tunnel angled gently down, disappearing into an inky blackness. With Dusk in the lead the two set off, following the tunnel to the right.

After ten minutes of walking a faint light began to glimmer ahead. They reached the end of the natural tunnel and found that a man-made tunnel continued it onwards. Man-height and two shoulder-widths wide, it was from this new section of tunnel that the light came. It flowed out between thick, heavy wooden props which held overhead beams in position, but its source was hidden by a curve in the tunnel. With enough light present for them to see by Dusk extinguished the lantern and they crept forward as silently as possible. Loose rock fragments crunched beneath their feet while all around them the wooden shoring gave out furtive creaks and groans as the weight of the mountain pressed down on it.

The tunnel, some fifty feet long, had finally merged into a small cave no more than twenty feet square and eight feet high. Here, on a slab of rock near the centre of the cave, sat a lantern. They paused on the threshold of the cave, peering cautiously in and Dusk drew his gun, thumbing the hammer back in a series of explosive clicks. If there was trouble waiting he wanted to be ready for it.

A figure sat slumped in one corner, half-hidden in the shadows. Crouching low the two eased forward. The figure moved in tired, exhausted slumber and the rattle of chains fell on Dusk's ears. Shock pulsed through him. Iron chains hobbled the figure's ankles and a further, longer section of chain ran from the centre of the hobble to an iron spike driven into the floor.

121

The figure moved, disturbed by their presence, lifting its head. Eyes in a gaunt, sore-encrusted face, squinted myopically in their direction. Sara let out a shocked scream and ran towards the figure.

'Tobe. Tobe, it's me, Sara,' she cried out as the pitiful figure cowered back raising thin, scab-covered fingers before its face.

Tobe Kellman dropped his hands as Sara fell to her knees before him.

'Sara?' His voice was barely above a whisper.

'Oh, my God. What has he done to you?' She reached out and gently gripped his painfully thin wrists.

'Sara?' Tobe Kellman croaked again and fear filled his eyes as the shadow of Dusk fell across him.

'It's all right, Tobe. He's a friend. He helped find you.' Tears filled her eyes at the pitiful, wasted figure of her once strong, robust brother.

'We'll get you outta here,' Dusk promised softly.

The terror grew in Tobe Kellman's eyes. 'Get away before he finds you. Run, run. He'll keep you here until you die.'

Dusk hunkered down beside Tobe Kellman.

'Why is he keeping you here, Tobe?'

'Frank and Mort died. Now there's only me left to dig, dig for Brogan's gold.' Tobe's voice strengthened as he spoke.

'Well, now you got company, boy. Family. Ain't that nice.' The jeering voice brought Dusk to his feet and he spun to face Cajun Bokes, who stood there with a shotgun aimed at them and a dark, leering smile on his face. 'Figured you for the nosy type, Landers.

Been keeping an' eye on the mine. Found your slickers, but then I guess you found a thing or two in the canyon.' He chuckled. 'Never no mind. You won't be telling on ol' Cajun Bokes. Now shuck the iron, boy. I can't miss wi' this ol' girl, an' I'll use it, make no mistake. Thumb an' finger real gentle like an' 'member, any fancy moves'll get you dead.'

Tight-lipped, Dusk did as he was told and let the gun drop.

'What in tarnation's going on here, Bokes, an' what's all this fool notion 'bout Brogan's gold?'

'T'ain't no fool notion, boy, it's here all right an' I should know, I put it here ten years ago,' Bokes said calmly.

CHAPTER 11

Dusk stared at Bokes, not believing what he was hearing.

'I don't understand.'

'Ain't too difficult. Brogan stole the gold in the first place an' then I stole it from him.' Bokes gave a chuckle. 'Brogan was shot up pretty bad when I happened on him. Fact is, he was dying, so I put him outta his misery an' pain an' found I had a wagon full o' gold on my hands. I knew there was a posse hunting him so I had to do somethin' wi' the gold real quick, if'n I was to keep it.

'I knew o' a big ol' cavern wi' a tunnel entrance jus' wide enough to take the wagon. I drove it in there an' blew up the entrance. Figured I'd let the hue an' cry die down. Six months, a year. I could wait an' the gold wasn't going anywhere. Trouble was that I hadn't reckoned on this ornery mountain. When I tried to dig out the tunnel entrance the mountain wouldn't let me. Kept on collapsing it back agin.

'In the end I figured out a new plan. I couldn't get to the gold from the top so I'd try from the bottom.

You see this mine is 'bout half a mile from where I hid the gold an' it had a natural tunnel pointing to where the gold was waiting. Reckoned I was half-way there already an' it was just a case o' blasting my way through, but the damn mountain didn't like it. You ever heard it said that this mountain was cursed, boy?' He stared at Dusk.

'Mostly from you as I recall,' Dusk replied coldly. 'What's that got to do wi' this fella an' those others out at Echo Canyon?'

'Everythin', boy. The mountain don' like people blasting away at its insides. It gets real feisty an' tunnels it ain't made itsel' it fills up wi' rock. Man gotta dig his way in an' then shore it up as he goes an' that sure is a lotta digging for one man.' Bokes nodded at his own words.

Dusk gave Bokes a horrified stare. 'You took men prisoners an' made them work in your mine?' He almost didn't believe what he was saying.

'Weren't too much of a chore. Gi'em grub an' plenty of whiskey, an' when they woke up . . .'

'You had 'em in chains down here,' Dusk completed.

'Work or die. It was up to them,' Bokes said callously.

'Shouldn't that have been work and die?' Dusk cut back sarcastically.

'They wanted Brogan's gold so I gave them the chance. I always warned 'em off coming on to the mountain to look for the gold. Tol' 'em to keep away, but they jus' kept a-coming. I think that was mighty fair of me.' Bokes smirked.

'Why'd you have to kill the horses, Bokes?'

'Weren't no good to me. Hadda get rid of 'em. Didn't think anyone'd find 'em. That was smart of you, boy. Have to do somethin' 'bout that. Mebbe a little blasting in Echo Canyon, once I've got rid of yours.'

'And us?'

'Got me some more workers. You see I figure the gold's pretty close now. Taken me ten years an' I can smell it.'

'You can't put the woman to work,' Dusk said hotly.

'She can wield a pick same as a man. If'n she can't then she ain't no use to me,' Bokes pointed out chillingly.

Dusk tensed himself, but Bokes caught the change.

'You wanna be a hero, Dusk Landers, then you'll be a dead one,' he warned.

Dusk knew that Bokes was right. The distance between them was too great to try and jump him. He'd be gunned down before he took two steps.

Sara left her brother's side and moved beside Dusk. 'I'll be all right, Dusk,' she said.

'Ain't that jus' dandy,' Bokes crowed, 'but I'll get me a little insurance as you look a mite feisty. Get over here, girl.'

'You leave her be, Bokes,' Dusk said sharply.

'I'll be OK, Dusk,' Sara said and at the same time he felt her hand steal about his lower back where Joe Little Wolf's sheathed knife protruded from his belt. She pulled the knife out and Dusk gave her a quick, anxious glance. She gave him a quick smile in return.

'Move it, girl,' Bokes ordered, 'an' don' get between us or you'll be the first to die. Move to the side, boy, two steps an' keep them hands high.' Dusk moved away from Sara who now stood with her hands behind her back. 'Come forward, girl.'

'You won't get away wi' this, Bokes,' Dusk spoke up, to get the other's attention away from Sara.

'I have for ten years, boy. This is my world up here an' soon I'll be away wi' the gold.'

'If'n the mountain lets you,' Dusk replied darkly. 'Mebbe the gold is cursed. Ain't that what you tell folks? Mebbe that's more true than you think.'

Cajun Bokes laughed. 'Jus' a story, boy, jus' a story.' The knife held behind Sara's back seemed to glow and flash with a brilliance as the light from the lamp touched it. Dusk swallowed on a suddenly dry throat and his heart began to pump faster behind his ribcage.

'You're a fool, Bokes. A mad, crazy fool,' he taunted hoarsely. Sara was close enough now to use the knife, if she could. It's one thing to think of killing a man, but something entirely different to do it. He had to distract Bokes enough to allow her the chance. 'Mebbe I'll take my chances against you, Bokes. You're not gonna chain me up in here!' Dusk finished with a shout and took a step forward, lowering his arms.

Bokes swung the shotgun up and his finger began to tighten on the trigger. In that instant Sara lunged with the knife driving the keen blade into Bokes' chest. The blade, instead of piercing his heart was deflected by the ribs and sliced through the flesh and muscle of his upper chest leaving a deep, six-inch-long gash in its wake.

Blood exploded on the front of Bokes' shirt. He let out a wild cry and freed one hand from the shotgun, as he staggered and half-turned, lashing out at her. His heavy, gnarled fist caught her across the mouth in a blow that sent her reeling sideways before she could get in another knife lunge. The knife spun from her hand as she went down, clanging as it hit the floor.

Before Bokes' fist caught her, Dusk was already flying forward and as Sara went down he rammed into the wounded Bokes, pushing the barrel of the shotgun up between them until it pointed at the roof. His momentum carried them both into the tunnel. The shotgun went off with a deafening roar and heavy-gauge shot tore into one of the overhead beams, splitting it into two pieces as both men went to the floor, Dusk on top of Bokes.

Dusk dragged the shotgun from Bokes' hands and threw it aside. Bokes, dazed and hurt, offered little resistance as Dusk hauled him to his feet and swung a fist that sent the miner staggering back against a wooden prop. The prop creaked and moved and a shower of small rock-fragments dropped like a curtain between them. Dusk became aware of a rumbling noise overhead, rather like the soft, throaty purr of a panther about to spring.

Cajun Bokes recovered himself.

'The tunnel's caving in!' he yelled and, fight forgotten, lunged past Dusk back into the cave. Dusk followed a split second later. The soft purr became a harsh, grating growl that rose to a roar as the roof of the tunnel began to collapse. Roof beams splintered and the wooden props snapped as the tunnel roof, from the cave entrance and all the way back to where it began, collapsed. The floor of the cave shook and a thick, choking cloud of dust filled the cave.

Dusk grabbed Sara and hurried her across the cave to where her brother lay. The two cowered down over the prone body as the dust cloud enveloped them. The rumble and grate of the tumbling rocks filled their ears and battered their brains with noise. To Dusk, it sounded as though the mountain was laughing at them. The sound seemed to go on for ever, driving itself into their dazed brains, but gradually, as the collapse settled, the noise lessened until all they could hear was the chatter of tiny rock-fragments tumbling into cracks and crevices, filling every last gap and dashing any hope of escape.

Miraculously, the lamp still stood on its rock table, casting a feeble light through the dense, brown, choking dust cloud, but as the dust began to settle the light grew stronger. Dusk and Sara rose to their feet, coughing and spluttering, eyes watering, their clothes and hair thick with dust. Bokes staggered out of the murk clutching his knife-slashed chest with one hand and leaning against the wall with the other. He glared at the two with red, streaming eyes.

'I'm hurt bad,' he moaned. A chunk of rock dropped from the cave roof which was now criss-crossed with cracks, and clattered to the ground on the other side of the cave. The air was filled with stealthy sounds that came from the very rock itself as the weight of the mountain pressed down on the cave. The tunnel collapse had altered the surrounding structure of the cave, adding pressure where before none had existed.

Dusk eyed him without pity. 'You're still alive,' he pointed out.

Bokes peered up at the roof. 'Ain't none o' us gonna be for much longer.'

'Dusk, I can feel cold air,' Sara said excitedly. Turning his back on Bokes, Dusk moved closer to her and felt the ethereal touch of cool air on his cheek. They were standing close to the pick-gouged end wall and Dusk saw that a crack had appeared in the wall, angled from top to bottom. It was through this half-inch-wide split that the air came.

'Mebbe there is a way out,' he said and peered around until his eyes settled on a pair of pickaxes along with a second lantern, the latter sitting unlit on a wooden keg of kerosene, in the corner of the cave. In a few quick strides he caught up the pickaxes and returned to Sara's side.

'Get the other lantern lit, Sara.' He turned to Cajun Bokes and tossed a pickaxe at his feet. 'Grab that, Bokes. If'n we can break through the wall we might have a chance.'

'I tol' you, I'm hurtin'. I can't swing no pickaxe,' Bokes whined. Above their heads a huge section of the roof dropped a foot or so, then held.

'Bokes, we're running outta time,' Dusk urged and began to swing at the wall. Bokes, after a second or two, forgot his own troubles, took up the other pickaxe and joined Dusk filling the cave with the ring of metal on stone.

The slab in the roof grumbled out a warning as it dropped another few inches. By the time Sara had lit the other lantern the two had opened up a six-inch hole. They attacked it with renewed energy, enlarging the hole until it was big enough to crawl through. Beyond it lay an inky blackness.

'What about Tobe?' Sara asked. 'We can't get him out with those chains on.'

'How 'bout it, Bokes? You got the key to those padlocks?'

There were three padlocks: two at the ankles passing through the links to hold the hobble chain in position and the third attaching the tether chain to the centre of the hobble. Wordlessly Cajun Bokes fished a big key from a pocket and handed it to Dusk. As Dusk bent to the task of freeing Tobe, Bokes tensed, snatched the lantern from Sara's hand and pushed her roughly aside.

'You die if'n you want to,' he shouted and vanished through the hole.

Sara gave a startled scream as the lantern was snatched from her hand and she was pushed roughly aside.

'He's getting away, Dusk,' she called out.

'Let him go. Get the other lantern, we've gotta get outta here pronto.' Dusk paused long enough to retrieve his gun and return it to its holster before gently lifting Tobe Kellman to his feet. The explosive crack of rock fracturing filled the air and cascades of dust fell like ragged, torn curtains through the ever widening fissures in the roof.

Dusk sent Sara through the hole first with the lantern, Tobe followed slowly and last of all Dusk scrambled through: not a moment too soon. As he came to his feet beyond the cave the roof collapsed behind him with a rumbling, grating roar and spat a cloud of dust angrily in his wake before tons of rock sealed the hole for ever.

They found themselves in yet another tunnel that formed a rabbit warren of tunnels and caves that made up the crumbling heart of Hollow Mountain. A few minutes later they found the wagon.

It stood in the centre of a spacious cavern. The bones of four horses lay tangled in the leather traces. A rear wheel had collapsed and the wagon had tilted, depositing its crated contents on the uneven floor. A couple of the crates had broken open and spilled their contents: slim bars of gold that shimmered in the light of a solitary lantern that stood on the floor by the wagon. It was the lantern that Bokes had taken, but of the man himself there was no sign. At that moment they gave no thought to the elusive Bokes, for there before their startled eyes, a legend no more, lay Brogan's gold.

Gently Dusk sat Tope Kellman down on a rock and leaving Sara with him, walked towards the wagon, their own danger temporarily set aside in his mind. Brogan's remains lay in the back of the tilted wagon: a pitiful skeleton of bones covered in brittle, peeling, paper-thin flesh wrapped in the tatters of the clothes he had died in ten years ago when Cajun Bokes had sealed him in. Dusk's foot kicked a gold bar, sending it skittering up against a second. The sound jerked Dusk back to reality.

'Bokes, where are you?' His voice echoed in the surrounding darkness.

From his hiding-place behind a tumble of boulders in the shadows beyond the bones of the fallen horses, Cajun Bokes had watched the three enter. In his hands he held a Winchester rifle that had once belonged to Brogan. He had found it alongside the mummified remains of the dead outlaw. The magazine had been full and even after ten years of non-use the lever mechanism had worked with satisfying smoothness. They were after his gold and he was not about to let them take it.

He watched through narrowed eyes as Dusk approached the wagon and came to a halt, staring down at the scattered gold bars. Bokes lifted the rifle and sighted down the barrel. He had a clear view of Dusk and from this distance he could not miss. He had the insane desire to giggle, but stifled the sound that would have given his position away. Only Dusk Landers was armed. Once he had taken care of him, the girl and her brother would be easy and his gold would be safe.

From his kneeling position, elbows propped on the boulder, the rifle was steady in his hands. He heard Dusk call his name and smiled. The young man was standing still, peering around, waiting for an answer. Well, he was just about to get it. Gently, Bokes, the rifle aimed at Dusk's head, tightened his finger on the trigger and squeezed.

*

'Can you see him, Dusk?' Sara called out and at that moment Bokes fired at the unsuspecting Dusk.

The sound of the shot, magnified and repeated in a series of echoes, exploded through the cavern and hit their ears with the ferocity of a cannon. Dusk dropped to a crouch, drawing his weapon and thumbing the hammer back, staring wildly around. There was movement on the edge of his vision beyond the front of the wagon. He focused in, raising his gun as Cajun Bokes appeared on the edge of the light. The man moved with staggering, unco-ordinated steps. His right hand was missing, reduced to a gory, blood-pumping stump, but it was his face that made the hairs on the back of Dusk's neck prickle, for Cajun Bokes no longer had a face. The rifle had blown itself apart in his hands and metal fragments, like flying shrapnel had reduced his face to a grisly red mask.

Strips of flesh hung in crimson tatters from jaw and cheekbones from a head that showed more bone than flesh. The eyes and nose were gone and the forward part of the hairline, lifted as efficiently as though a scalping knife had been used and folded back over his head. Bokes' mouth gaped open in a scream that never came, tongue mashed and forced back down his ripped and lacerated throat as the sharp pieces of metal scoured the flesh from his face and drove into his brain through his eyes. Bokes took one last, faltering step and then toppled forward and lay still.

The echoes of Sara's scream still echoed in the cavern as Dusk turned away from the gruesome sight. How the man had ever managed those last few steps he would never know, but of one thing he was certain. The tale of cursed gold that Bokes had spoken of was no longer a tale in his mind. The gold was cursed and the thought sent a shiver down his spine.

'What happened to him?' Sara asked in a shocked whisper as Dusk reached her and Tobe.

'Figure the gun he used was one he found in the wagon.' Dusk gave an ugly laugh. 'I guess Brogan finally had his revenge on the man who sealed him in. Let's try an' find a way out of here.'

'What about the gold?'

'That can stay here and remain a legend. It's killed too many folk an' I don't aim to be its next victim,' Dusk responded grimly.

'This is hopeless, Dusk, we'll never get away from here,' Sara wailed as they paused to rest. There was dejection in her face and the slump of her tired shoulders said that she was ready to give in to the inevitable.

For what seemed hours they had struggled, crawled and slipped down dark tunnels, waded through icy water, only seeing what lay ahead in the limited glow of the lanterns. Sometimes they'd had to retrace their steps when they reached a dead end. Tired and exhausted from having to carry Tobe Kellman who lapsed more and more frequently into periods of unconsciousness, Dusk knew how she felt.

None of them had eaten in a while and he could feel his own strength waning, but he refused to give up. He ran a hand across his brow and forced a smile.

'We'll make it,' he said with more confidence than he felt.

'Will we, Dusk?' She sounded less than confident. Around them the drip and splash of water had become so much a part of their dark, claustrophobic world that it no longer registered on their tired brains.

'Sure we will,' he assured her. 'The next tunnel, the next bend.'

One of the lanterns began to splutter, the light it gave out flaring and dipping as the wick soaked up the last of the fuel in a desperate effort to stay alive. It sent flickering shadows dancing around them. The loss of light was Dusk's biggest fear. Without it they would be lost for ever in their subterranean world. The flickering lantern was a message to Dusk for them to get moving again. The other lantern still burnt with a strong and steady flame, but even that would not last for ever.

The guttering lantern finally winked out and Sara pressed a fist to her lips.

'Time to get moving,' Dusk said, forcing his aching body up. Tobe Kellman, in a period of wakefulness, tried to push Dusk aside as the other went to lift him.

'Leave me. I'll only hold you back. Get Sara out of here,' he croaked.

Sara fell to her knees at his side and gripped his hands.

'Don't be silly, Tobe. We're not going to leave you,' she said gently, then lifted a hand and stroked his hot, fevered brow and tried to hide the despair that engulfed her. Tobe was in a bad way. Fever had taken over his wasted, half-starved body, beading his ridged brow and sunken cheeks in fat pearls of sweat.

'You must,' he pleaded. 'For your own sake. You'll never make it out of here with me.'

'You let us worry 'bout that, Tobe. We came here looking for you an' now we've found you we sure ain't gonna leave you.' Dusk spoke up and Sara threw him a grateful look.

'We'll be out of here soon, you'll see,' Sara promised, forcing an encouraging smile while at the same time fighting back the tears that threatened to overwhelm her. Tobe was dying. Unless they got him out of here soon, Hollow Mountain would become his tomb.

There was a weird quality about the latest tunnel that they had stumbled into which had Dusk baffled. Its walls, roof and floor were strangely smooth and scored with gouges. But he had little time to reflect on its oddness for at the far end of the tunnel came a faint, pale glow. After setting Tobe down, he and Sara went forward to investigate and as they did so the glow vanished. But by now there was more to baffle the brain.

Where the tunnel ended lay a pile of bark-stripped branches and shattered tree-limbs, jammed and twisted together, rising from a bed of gravel and boulders. It was as though someone had come along with a large brush and swept all the debris into one corner, for the main body of the tunnel was clear.

'What do you make o' that?' Dusk said, mystified.

'That we are going to have to find another way out. This tunnel ends here,' Sara replied.

'Bring the lantern closer,' Dusk called softly. Something else had caught his eye. The walls, on closer inspection, were covered in a thin film of dust that fell away as he rubbed it. He shook his head. 'I don't get this. I've seen rock dust in all the caves an' tunnels we've been in, but this stuff looks like it's been painted on.' He rubbed the surface again and a sudden gust of wind swirled the dust in the lantern glow. Both felt its soft, cool touch and stared at each other in surprise.

At that moment the pale, ghostly glow that they had seen earlier returned and both turned their faces up in surprise. Above their heads the base of a round shaft appeared. It looked to be twenty, maybe twenty-five feet long and went straight up. The brightest source of the silver glow came from the top of the shaft. Dusk gazed up at it speechless for a moment until Sara cried out:

'It's moonlight, Dusk. It's the moon shining.' As the glow faded into darkness once more, she continued: 'Clouds blowing across the face of the moon causing the light to come and go. The storm must be over.'

Dusk nodded. Earlier they had heard distant, muted thunder rumbling in far-off caverns, but he had not heard it for some time now.

'Well if'n the moon can get in we can get out,'

Dusk announced, looking up. They were so near to escaping from Hollow Mountain and at the same time so far. It was as if the mountain was mocking them.

'How can we get up there?' Sara asked. The flame in the lamp spiked, dropped and came back to normal.

'I ain't figured it yet, but the lantern ain't gonna last much longer, so this is as far as we go.'

As they returned to where Tobe lay Dusk froze in his tracks and the hair on the nape of his neck rose. From the end of the tunnel where they had entered came a soft, hissing, scraping sound. A sound that he had heard only once in his life before: the night his father had died on Hollow Mountain!

CHAPTER 12

'Dusk. What is it?' Sara stared at him. He barely heard her as memories of that terrible night flashed through his mind. The huge mishappen head rising up from the shaft. His pa yelling for him to run. He knew what the sinister, rasping, hissing sound was. A picture leapt into his mind. That of a long, scaled, sinuous body slithering through the tunnels, its scales scraping along the walls, gouging the walls like those around him. . . . 'Dusk, what's the matter?' Sara tugged at his arm, alarm in her voice.

Dusk swallowed as the sound of her voice brought him back from the threshold of panic. Whatever was coming could not possibly be some huge snake. Reason told him that, but childhood memories coupled with the darkness and close confinement of the tunnel confused him.

'Just something I thought I'd never hear again,' he said thickly. 'Something that happened a long time ago.'

'The night your pa died,' she said, and he swung a frowning gaze on her. 'Joe told me what happened. I

– I hope you don't mind?'

'Don't matter much now,' he responded tautly. 'It's back an' it's coming.' He drew his gun as he spoke. His heart was hammering in his chest, throat dry as the supernatural terror gripped him.

The sound grew louder, more insistent, more menacing. In a final act of sheer bravado and to keep the lid on his own fear, he took the lantern from her hand and thumbing back the hammer of his gun started forward. If he was going to die he would rather meet it head on than stand meekly waiting.

'Dusk,' Sara called out, following in his wake.

'Stay with Tobe,' he called back over his shoulder, but she kept coming.

The lantern pushed the darkness away as Dusk went purposefully forward. As he approached the mouth of the tunnel that had opened into this one he stopped and his childhood terror flooded back. A huge grey, glistening head covered in lumps lurched through the opening. Sara screamed and Dusk fired twice in quick succession, the gunshots deafening in the confines of the tunnel.

The head seemed to fall forward as the bullets ploughed into it. Holes that should have streamed blood or ichor appeared briefly then closed up. As the head went down more of the creature's body oozed after it in a thick, grey coil. The flame in the lantern chose that moment to dim. Dark, flickering shadows leapt protectively forward to cover the huge creature. It hissed and scraped in its protective shroud of darkness and Sara grabbed Dusk's arm.

142

'Stop shooting, Dusk. It's mud. It's not alive. It's a river of mud!'

The words hit Dusk's brain. 'Mud!' he repeated stupidly.

She darted past him, dipped her fingers into the ooze and returned to his side holding her grey, glistening finger out before his face. 'The rain has forced it down the tunnels. It's carrying rocks and boulders with it. That's what is making the sound, the scraping sound.'

'Mud!' Dusk said again, feeling the cool stickiness that coated her fingers and as the lantern flame steadied itself he looked anew at his childhood nightmare, seeing for the first time the reality behind the myth his mind had conjured. The mud had now spread out across the floor and was starting to creep towards them as more flowed in.

'Mud!' He wanted to laugh. He had spent his growing-up years terrified by mud. Half-blinded by the rain and lit by flashes of lightning, he had mistaken a column of mud, forced up from below, as the mythical snake god. In a flash of clear thinking the eyes that he had seen all those years ago had been small boulders, the mouth most likely a section of tree with perhaps a couple of branches that looked like huge fangs.

The tide of mud plopped and gurgled and boulders grated as they were rolled along. He knew then that the gouges in the wall had been made by the rocks carried within the river of mud, rubbing along the walls of the tunnel as it filled. The river of mud had deposited the tangle of tree limbs and heavier boulders before its climb up the shaft. The strange coating on the walls was the dried remains from the last time the river of mud had flowed this way.

The relief of learning the truth after all these years was tempered by the very real danger that now threatened them: a danger far worse than some legendary snake god. They were trapped and the way the mud was oozing in would soon fill the tunnel and draw them into its cold, grey, suffocating heart. Tobe Kellman had struggled up on to his elbows at the sound of the shots.

'What was that shooting?' he asked.

'I just killed a demon that's been haunting me some for a whole heap o' years,' Dusk replied sheepishly and at Tobe's questioning gaze gave a snorting laugh. 'I'll tell you 'bout it later. First we gotta get outta here.'

'Easier said than done,' Sara cut back.

They moved down the tunnel to its end where the tangle of branches and boulders littered the area beneath the shaft. Dusk sat Tobe down and stared up at the shaft a foot or so above his head, trying to think against the plop and gurgle of the mud closing in behind them. His eyes strayed around, at the pale circle of Sara's face to Tobe's drooping head; at the bone-white branches gripped between the boulders.

'We're trapped, Dusk. The only way out is the shaft and there's no way we can climb that,' she said dejectedly. They had come so far against impossible odds only to end up trapped by the mud that was crawling steadily towards them. Small boulders scraped and rubbed together as they were carried along by the thick, oily, oozing mass. The only thing in their favour was that the tunnel sloped gently down from where they stood, temporarily slowing the approach of the mud but only postponing the inevitable.

'Mebbe not,' Dusk said thoughtfully glancing up the shaft once again. It was roughly circular and close to three feet in diameter. A note of excitement in his voice made her look intently at his upturned face. He was smiling and without a further word of explanation he began to examine the branches, pulling out those that were as thick as his forearm.

'What are you doing, Dusk?' she wanted to know.

'You'll see. Ain't too sure it'll work, but if'n it does . . .' Without another word to satisfy her curiosity he took a length of branch, leapt up on to the large boulder and was able to get his head and shoulders into the shaft. There was enough room for him to feed the branch into the shaft and raise it over his head. The branch was a little longer than the width of the shaft, but by placing one end of the branch against one side of the shaft wall and then pulling down on the other until it jammed and held firm, he had the first rung of a rudimentary ladder in place. To test it he took a hold with both hands and pulled himself up until his feet were clear of the boulder and hung there for a few seconds. The higher end of the branch slipped down an inch or so and held firmer than before. As he dropped back into the tunnel he was smiling.

'Get enough o' those in position then we'll be able to climb clear outta here. Now I'm gonna get up on

145

to that first one. When I call climb up on to the boulder an' pass me the next branch, one up from those half a dozen I've pulled out.'

'Will it work?' she asked doubtfully.

'We'll die trying,' he said with dark humour. He clambered back on to the boulder and she watched his feet disappear from sight.

In the shaft Dusk managed to haul himself up on to the branch using the shaft walls to support himself. It proved a tight squeeze wriggling between the branch and the wall, but at last he was there, crouching with his feet on the branch. It creaked a little beneath his weight but held. He called down for Sara to pass him the next one and this he jammed across the shaft at waist level as he stood on the first rung of an improvised ladder.

He worked quickly, climbing up to get the next in position before returning to the lowest rung to get another branch. It grew hot in the confines of the shaft as he worked. His body ached. His shoulders were sore from being scraped along the shaft walls, but adrenalin kept him going. Finally he jammed the last branch into position a few inches below the top of the shaft and climbed up enough for his head and shoulders to emerge into a big cave. Ahead a wide opening gave him a view of the tops of night-shrouded pines, silvered by an unseen moon. Cool, pine-scented air filled his nostrils and he felt like whooping for joy. Taking a deep breath he clambered back down the shaft, from one uneven rung to the other, for none of the branches was level.

He rejoined Sara in the tunnel and became aware

of a new noise: a deep rumble and grind. In the light of the lantern, which was now flickering its last few gasps, he saw a huge boulder nearly half the width of the tunnel being slowly pushed along by the main body of mud behind it. Mud squeezed around the edges and oozed over the top, lubricating it as it rolled slowly towards them, pushing a tide of mud before it. Too heavy to be carried up the shaft, it would join the others below. In time the tunnel would become blocked.

'I've seen the trees, smelt the good air. It's just a short climb, Sara,' he cried.

Sara grabbed Dusk's arm urgently. 'What about Tobe? He'll never be able to climb it,' she whispered fiercely and Dusk shot the man a glance. His escape route had not taken into account Tobe's weak, semi-conscious condition. He ran a hand across his lips.

'I'll think o' something,' he promised. 'You go first. Leave the lamp.'

'I'm not leaving Tobe behind.'

'For God's sake, woman, we haven't got much time,' he snapped roughly and she stepped back as though he had slapped her across the cheek. 'Please, Sara.' There was a begging note in his voice.

'Do it, sis. Do it for me.' Tobe Kellman spoke up, enjoying a brief moment of lucidity.

She eyed them both and then nodded, tight-lipped, and clambered on to the boulder. She could-n't quite reach the first branch until Dusk jumped up beside her and lifted her, then pushed her feet up into the shaft. After that she was on her own.

'Shout when you reach the top,' Dusk called up

after her. He watched her progress up the makeshift ladder with anxious eyes; a dark shadow against the pale, icy light of the moon. 'How are you doing, Sara?'

'Nearly there,' came the breathless reply and then a few minutes later. 'I've made it.'

'We're coming up,' Dusk shouted back and turned to the seated Tobe who was still conscious and eyeing him with bright, fevered eyes.

'I'll never make it, Dusk. We both know that. I'm obliged to you for saving sis. Now save yourself.'

Dusk eyed the approaching boulder in the guttering light of the lantern, the edge of the leading mud surge now within yards of the two of them, and sniffed.

'I've been shot at, near drowned, left for dead, almost crushed to death and walked for miles through goddam tunnels in this worm-eaten mountain an' all because o' that pig-headed sister o' yours. But what's happened so far will be nothing to what'll happen if'n I climb outta that shaft wi'out you an' I ain't that brave, so let's get moving.'

Tobe suddenly grinned. It was the first time Dusk had seen the expression on the young man's face and it gave his thin, wasted features a boyish look.

'She is kinda pushy, though, ain't she!' he remarked and both men laughed.

The journey up the shaft was a nightmare for Dusk. Sitting, legs astride the first rung as close to one end as possible with the walls of the shaft supporting him, he was able to reach down and grip Tobe's hands. The boy had found the strength to stand on the boulder and stretch his arms up and Dusk had hauled him up. The problem now was that the wedged branches were taking the weight of two. With Tobe sitting on the branch and leaning back against the wall, Dusk struggled into a standing position. The branch creaked ominously and one end began to splinter and slide down the wall. To make matters worse the lantern had finally died, plunging them into darkness relieved only by the moonlight above, which did not reach them.

Praying that Tobe would remain conscious Dusk clambered on to the second branch and gripping the one above was able to reach down with one hand, find Tobe's hands in the dark and haul him up, glad that the young man's weight was lighter than normal. Even so, his arms felt as though they were being pulled out of their sockets.

The branch rungs protested noisily. There were six in all, but so far they were holding. Below them, unseen in the darkness, the big boulder had been pushed aside. The river of mud now filled the lower tunnel and was starting to ooze up the shaft. Dusk could hear it, gurgling and hissing and making plopping noises as bubbles of air exploded on the surface. Though he could not see it, he could hear that it was getting close.

Four rungs, five rungs. They were now in the reflected moonglow only a few feet from the top and Dusk felt drained. He had his arm about Tobe's waist as the two stood on the fifth rung when the little help that Tobe could give went and Dusk felt the other become a dead weight in his grip.

'Tobe, Tobe,' he croaked.

'What's happening?' Sara called down.

'He's passed out,' Dusk said through gritted teeth. Beneath his feet he could feel the branch bending and making disturbing cracking sounds. He looped one arm over the top rung and wrapped the other tightly around Tobe's waist. Sweat rolled down his face and blurred his vision, his heart racing with the effort. Tobe's chest was against the upper rung, head lolling forward. Dusk managed to hook Tobe's arms over the rung and the unconscious Tobe hung there, legs buckling on the rung below. It was then that the rung Dusk stood on snapped. He grabbed the upper rung to save himself from falling.

His heart leapt into his mouth as he hung there and felt his feet dip into something thick and gelatinous. The mud was rising fast. The rung he clung to shifted at one end, scraping with a harsh splintering sound against the shaft wall. It held but was beginning to bend.

'Dusk, hurry,' Sara shrilled down. It was a command he needed no reminding of. Gritting his teeth he braced his feet on tiny wrinkles in the rock face on either side of the shaft and hauled himself up. His arm and shoulder muscles were exploding with pain. He knew he had reached his limit and his strength was ebbing fast, but doggedly he kept going until his head and shoulders were above the mouth of the shaft. With an effort he got his knees on to the rung and with Sara's help, hauled himself out of the shaft.

His whole body was trembling with fatigue as he

rolled himself over into a sitting position, braced his feet on the rung and reached down for Tobe. The young man still hung there, but was starting to slip down, his feet held in the grip of the rising mud. Dusk got his fingers under Tobe's armpits, heaved and at the same time pushed down with his feet against the creaking rung. The mud protested with a soft, sucking sound as Tobe's feet came clear and Dusk hauled him free of the shaft, collapsing back with Tobe on top of him. Sara helped Dusk roll the still unconscious Tobe to one side then Dusk staggered to his feet.

Sara flew at Dusk, almost knocking him over in her joy.

'You did it, Dusk, you did it.' She was laughing and crying all at the same time.

'Whoa, girl, we're not outta danger yet,' Dusk said with a breathless laugh. To prove his point the rising mud reared up out of the shaft and collapsed around its edges. More followed. 'We 'uns need to get outta here, get to higher ground.' With Sara helping, Dusk half-carried, half-dragged Tobe Kellman from the cave into the cool, night air. There was a wide ledge to the left of the cave entrance above which a steep bank of pine rose. Dusk indicated it with his head.

'Up there,' he gasped to Sara and she nodded. Five minutes later Dusk lay gratefully on his back. The coldness of the rain-washed rock seeped into his body, driving out the fire from his aching joints and muscles.

In the moonlight below them the river of mud surged from the cave, gleaming like mercury in the frosty glow of the moon. It rolled down the slope away from the cave, hissing and gurgling, its thick, soft body lumpy with the rocks and small boulders that it carried.

Dusk managed to sit up, groaning with the effort. He looked across at Sara who was tending her brother. 'How is he?' he called across.

'Unconscious but still alive. You saved his life, Dusk.'

'That's what you paid me for. Now what was it. Twenty dollars, but you could go to thirty.' Dusk said lightly reminding her of their first ever conversation. He rose to his feet and laughed at the look on Sara's face. 'Just' kidding, ma'am.' His legs felt as boneless as the river of mud below them. 'Reckon it'll be sun-up in an hour or so.' He peered around.

Something crashed about in the dark blanket of pines above the ledge. Probably an animal, but his mind was distracted as he took in their surroundings. The place was familiar. The cave was the very one he and his father had sheltered in on that fateful night when the snake and had been born in his mind.

There was a further crashing in the undergrowth much closer than beforehand, and Dusk turned, tension tearing through his body as Sara screamed, 'Dusk, look out!'

A bulky shadow appeared before him. He glimpsed something swinging towards him as he made to draw his gun and he threw up a protective arm. A thick length of tree limb wielded in shadowy hands crashed against his upraised arm. He heard the snap of breaking bone and pain flared from wrist to elbow. He staggered back, slipped and went to his knees, a cry escaping from his lips. His other hand came up, fisting his gun and a booted foot slammed into his wrist, numbing it and sending the gun flying from his grasp. He heard it clatter and bounce on the rock somewhere behind him. Dusk peered up and before him stood . . .

'Gonna kill me a dead man. Now ain't that some-thin'?' The bearded face of Coot Lacey loomed over Dusk and the eyes in the moon-silvered face glowed with the light of madness. 'You figured you'd done killed me, eh, boy?' Coot's face contorted in a crazy laugh. Spittle gleamed on his bearded lips as he threw aside the makeshift club and drew a knife that shone with white fire in the moonlight. 'Mebbe you did kill me, boy, but you was dead when you did it, so that makes us both dead, ain't that a pure fact?' Coot broke into another peal of harsh, chuckling laughter.

Dusk stared up dazedly at the man who he had thought was dead.

'Gonna cut your heart out, boy,' Coot sang out happily and raised the knife.

A shot rang out and a bullet smashed into Coot's chest, staggering him back with a look of surprise on his face. He recovered and surged forward. A second shot broke the silence of the night and the left side of Coot's face blew apart taking part of the skull with it. Blood, leached of colour by the moonlight, jetted blackly from the wound. Coot spun, still clutching the knife and toppled sideways from the ledge into the rolling river of mud below.

Dusk snapped his head around. Sara stood there holding out the smoking gun with both hands. She dropped it and ran to Dusk's side.

'I thought he was dead,' she moaned.

'He is now,' Dusk replied as he climbed unsteadily to his feet. 'Think my arm's bruk.' He held his arm tightly across his chest and looked towards the cave and the mountain rearing above it. 'I hope this damn mountain ain't got any more surprises.'

But it still had one left.

In the first light of dawn that cracked the sky less than an hour after their escape from the cave, Dusk stared down at the course the river of mud had taken. It had long since ceased to ooze and run from the cave mouth. Now it resembled a thick, grey slick of slime rather like that left by a snail. Its wide path was littered with rocks and boulders that it had dragged from the depths of the mountain.

Later, when the sun came up, it would harden, and in time turn to dust which the mountain winds would whisk away until nothing of it remained. The body of Coot Lacey had been carried away to the edge of the plateau where it had fallen into a deep gorge beyond.

In the growing light of day the still damp path of the river of mud, beside the debris of rocks and boulders carried up from deep within the mountain, was littered with oblong shapes, all the same size. Curiosity made Dusk climb down from the ledge. He retrieved one such shape, picked it up, and rubbed it against the leg of his pants. The revealed surface glowed with a rich, golden hue and he gave a bitter laugh. After all the years and the many deaths, the mountain had finally given up Brogan's gold.